By buying this book you are directly supporting the mission of Green Card Voices.

“This deeply moving book is a priceless project. It not only helps the student writers to share their stories, it also enriches the lives of those who read it…other students, teachers, administrators, and people in the community. This is a perfect example of how our students become our teachers. Thank you to everyone who has shared their experiences and stories to help us all learn and grow.”

—Jo Anne L. Antonacci, District Superintendent, Monroe 2-Orleans Board of Cooperative Educational Services

"We are all so fortunate that these young individuals have chosen to share their stories with us. Their bravery should be an inspiration to us all."

—David A. Rivera, Council Majority Leader, Niagara District, Buffalo Common Council

“I am grateful to Green Card Voices for continuing to bring us the gift of student stories—this time in upstate New York. The stories, photographs, and videos allow us to listen to and learn from immigrant youth. Their narratives go beyond labels and statistics to humanize the wide range of immigrant experiences that are often excluded from discussions and debates on immigration.”

—Tatyana Kleyn, EdD, Associate Professor, The City College of New York and Principal Investigator, The CUNY Initiative on Immigration and Education (CUNY-IIE)

“*Green Card Youth Voices: Upstate New York* is a compelling and profound glimpse into the lives of young immigrants who have lived extraordinary lives. Their experiences of life before and after immigration give tremendous insight to the current human condition. This is a must-read for anyone seeking to develop a more global perspective of 21st-Century living.”

—Patricia Uttaro, Director, Rochester Public Library & Monroe County Library System

“The words of the young immigrants featured in *Green Card Youth Voices: Upstate New York* inspire us with their enthusiasm for their educations and opportunities, their abilities to overcome challenges, and their desires to contribute to their communities—reminding us of the promise and potential they offer to our society.”

—Donna Gitter, JD, Professor of Law, Baruch College/Zicklin School of Business, The City University of New York

“There is no question that there are members of our community who are voiceless and therefore underrepresented, including immigrants. To give voices to underrepresented but valuable human-beings who bring culture, diversity, and perspective to our community will surely spread empathy and enrich our community for generations to come. The voices we hear through the stories of our neighbors in the *Green Card Voices Youth Voices: Upstate New York book* are honest, revealing, and touching. This collection is a must-read for everyone!”

—Gary Baier, ENL/ELA Teacher, Fairport Central School District

“This book is priceless. As a lifelong Western New York resident—and as a hardcore true Buffalonian—your effort is truly heroic and inspiring. Buffalo is truly the City of Good Neighbors, and Rochester is appropriately named 'Flower City.' It is ironic that it is in these cities that this class of student immigrants has arrived and set only the highest of goals for themselves. This book is a must-read for anyone and everyone interested in learning about the world around them, the life and death issues that children face on a daily basis, and how fortunate we are to live in America where we have the opportunity to share our resources, not the least of which are ample food and water.”

—Sareer A. Fazili, Esq, Immediate Past President of the Board of Directors and Council Member, Islamic Center of Rochester and Barakah Muslim Charity

"Kudos to these new speakers of English for sharing their stories in their authentic voices. They bring us the gifts of their fluency in their home languages, their tenacity, dedication, and their high hopes for the future. Their resilience can only make our communities stronger."

—Cindy McPhail, PhD, Professor and Associate Dean for Academic Affairs, School of Education and Director of the Bilingual Extension Program, Nazareth College

"As educators in the 21st century, we recognize the importance of amplifying diverse student voices. I am proud to see our bilingual learners featured in *Green Card Youth Voices: Upstate New York*. Their journeys to Upstate New York and their experiences as bilingual students in a new community are stories that capture the resiliency of a people and the faithfulness of a village. Thank you to Green Card Voices for capturing their personal stories."

—Analy Cruz-Phommany, Director of Bilingual Education, Rochester City School District

"*Green Card Youth Voices: Upstate New York* provides our refugee and immigrant students with a platform to AMPLIFY their voices. The stories of strength and resilience depicted in this book connect refugees and immigrants to their communities through multimedia storytelling highlighting the common thread that unites them all."

—Gliset Colón, PhD, Assistant Professor, Exceptional Education Department and Coordinator, Bilingual Certificate Program, Buffalo State, The State University of New York

"The personal stories of these immigrant adolescents paint a poignant picture of their life experiences, and how the move to the U.S. has impacted them in a variety of profound ways. It's so important in the midst of national debate about immigration to hear the voices of young people, including those from one of the schools we support, Lafayette International High School in Buffalo. All of these young people have immigrated for a variety of reasons and their personal stories provide insights into both the hurdles they've had to surmount and the positive role they are already playing in their communities, families, and schools. Bravo!"

—Claire E. Sylvan, EdD, Founder and Senior Strategic Adviser, Internationals Network for Public Schools

"*Green Card Youth Voices: Upstate New York*, a collection of stories from students in the Rochester/Upstate New York area, gives a glimpse into the difficulties faced by young people whose families have chosen to migrate to the U.S. and leave family members and friends behind. To be a refugee means to enter a strange country, to learn a new language, to find a place to live and to work. Young people are especially challenged to find acceptance in their new homeland and new schools. This book gives a glimpse at some of these young people who are finding a place in their new homeland and can begin to dream of a future for themselves. Hopefully this book will become a good resource for educators and those who are interested in working with refugees and assisting them to adjust to their new homeland.

—Sister Phyllis Tierney, Coordinator, Sisters of St. Joseph Justice and Peace Office Sisters of Saint Joseph of Rochester

"Hipocampo Children's Books, Rochester, New York's Woman/Latinx Indie, congratulates the students from Rochester and Buffalo, New York, who share their stories in *Green Card Youth Voices: Upstate New York*. We believe in the transformative power of translanguaging and celebration of cultures. The stories in this Green Card Voices book will both serve to empower the speaker and listener while releasing the power of imagination."

—Henry Padrón, Co-Owner, Hipocampo Children's Books, Rochester, New York

ISBN 13: 978-1-949523-16-4
eISBN 13: 978-1-949523-19-5
LCCN: 2018932723

Printed in the United States of America
First Printing: 2021
20 19 18 17 16 5 4 3 2 1

Edited by Tea Rozman and Julie Vang

Cover design by Elena Dodevska and Shiney Chi-Ia Her
Interior design by Shiney Chi-Ia Her

Photography, videography by Media Active: Youth Produced Media

Green Card Voices
2611 1st Avenue South
Minneapolis, MN 55408
www.greencardvoices.org

Consortium Book Sales & Distribution
34 Thirteenth Avenue NE, Suite 101
Minneapolis, MN 55413-1007
www.cbsd.com

Green Card Youth Voices

Immigration Stories from Upstate New York High Schools

Stela Ciko, Alex Tsipenyuk, Esma Okutan, Ayşe, Stivia Jorgji, Katsiaryna Liavanava, Sultan Yahya, Mysstorah Shaibi, Abdulmageed Shaibi, Gunasekera Subasinghe, Zadquiel Jose Ortiz Lopez, Yanielys Marie Nieves Rivera, Sebastian Antonio Berdecia Negron, Jeffrey Omar Cruz, Wanlee Arys Irizarry Pacheco, Bryant Pagan, Anika Khanam, Estel Neema, Sekuye Bolende, Jonnoto Nor Ahmad, Zainab, Muna Ismael, Abdishakur Luhizo, Immaculee Mukeshimana, Flavia Kayitesi, Mireille & Mery Nabukomborwa, Manea Almadrahi, Ca Arrive Rushikana

Authors

Julie Vang and Tea Rozman
Editors

We dedicate this book to the thirty immigrants, colonial refugees, climate refugees, and refugees fleeing conflict whose stories conveyed in this book are so brave. It is our hope that you stay safe and healthy in the midst of the COVID-19 pandemic, find a sense of belonging despite undergoing distance learning that brought isolation and slowed the process of integration.

Our hearts go out especially to the Asian communities who have experienced increased xenophobia and other people of color who have been discriminated against during this challenging time.

Table of Contents

How to Use this Book

At the end of each student's essay, you will find a URL link to that student's digital narrative on Green Card Voices' website. You will also see a QR code link to that story. Below are instructions for using your mobile device to scan a QR code.

1. Open your phone camera and scan the QR code. If your phone camera cannot scan the code, using your mobile device—such as a smartphone or tablet—visit the App Store for your network, such as the Apple Store or the Android Store. Search the App Store for a "QR reader." You will find multiple free apps for you to download, and any one of them will work with this book.

2. Open your new QR reader app. Once the app has opened, hover the camera on your mobile device a few inches away from the QR code you want to scan. The app will capture the image of the QR code and take you to that student's profile page on the Green Card Voices website.

3. Once your web browser opens, you'll see the digital story. Press play and watch one of our inspirational stories.

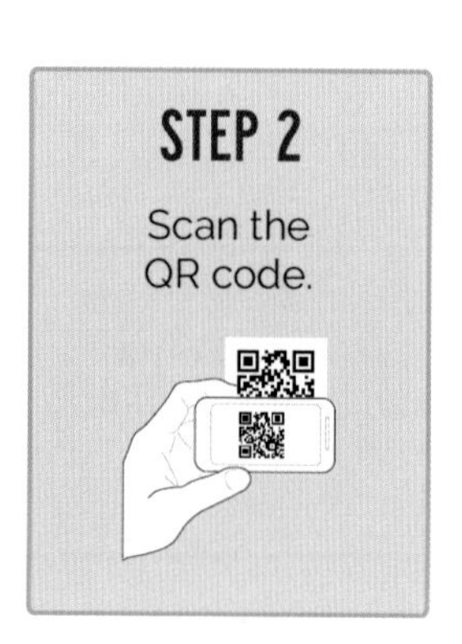

STEP 2
Scan the QR code.

STEP 3
Watch the digital story.

Foreword

I and the authors of this book are just a few of the millions of immigrants and refugees that have come to the United States of America over the course of many decades and who now proudly call America their home. I have read and am in awe of the stories and everything these young people have gone through in their short lives. I am excited for you, the reader, to embark on the journey of discovery. In the following pages you will meet your current neighbors, your future college classmates, your future coworkers. The future leaders of your community—their children might go to preschool with your children—get to know them.

We are your neighbors.

My dad has lived in America since 1989, ten years before I was born. At the end of 2011, my family started the process of immigrating to America. First, my dad took my two brothers and two sisters to America while I stayed in Yemen with my mom until she received her visa. In December of 2012, we arrived in Rochester, New York, and after a very long time my family was finally reunited. I was so touched when I read that one of the authors, Ca Arrive, too got reunited with his father. Only in his case he didn't see his dad for 10 years! Did you know family reunification is one of the major reasons why people migrate? My story and the stories you are about to read are full of heartbreak, abandonment, loneliness, and they are also stories of sacrifice, difficult decisions, and joyous reunions.

Having to learn English is also one of the major connecting points with me and the authors of this book. Some of them had to learn more than one additional language! Muna, one of the authors, was born in Somalia, and when her family fled to Ethiopia, she had to learn Amharic to continue her education. Upon arrival to the U.S. she had to learn her third language—English. I am so excited and proud of the authors in this book for not only learning English in a short amount of time but now also becoming published authors.

I spoke no English upon arrival in Rochester, New York, but I soon started attending Rochester International Academy to learn English and other subjects. In two years, I developed the mentality to put all of my effort into learning English. I was determined to become fluent. Everywhere I encountered an English word, I tried to pronounce it. I watched videos and talked to others with my broken English, so that I could speak English sooner. I would spend hours just reading and studying because I knew how important education was. Every time I got a B+, I cried because I knew that I didn't put all of my effort into getting a better grade. After a year and a half of learning, I was able to pass my first two Regents Exams in English. Even though I didn't get good scores on them, I was very impressed with my strength and my study habits. It was the moment that I realized I was able to reach my goals.

I was proud of all my hard work, because to me education is life. It's the key to open the doors to my future—the future that not many Yemeni girls have. Thankfully, I am from a family that honors education, but I didn't come from a country that believes in education for girls. When I was in my country, I always worked hard just to prove people wrong and show that every girl wants to go to school. Not a lot of people understood my passion for learning because in Yemen nothing comes before rules and traditions—including education. Yet even as a young child, I was fighting for change and women's rights. Passing the Regents Exams in English made me want to reach more goals. America gave my dreams a new meaning. In 2015, I transfered to the World of Inquiry School as a sophomore. I continued to excel in school and was placed in honors and AP classes.

Education is one of the major reasons why people migrate. Mery and Mireille, Congolese sisters who lived in very difficult circumstances in a refugee camp Muyiga Gasogwe in Burundi, write about the poor education they received in the camp, and how grateful they are to get a good education in America. Anika from Bangladesh writes about school simply being not good at all, especially the public one. And Gunasekera writes about how in Sri Lanka you would get hit by teachers if you didn't do your homework or if you didn't pay attention in class. Their and my stories, which you are about to read, are full of deep commitment to education, hard work and dedication from the students and their parents alike.

After living in America for a while, I realized that despite learning English and being a good student, people treated me differently because of my hijab. This made me feel disconnected in my new home, until I learned about World Hijab Day. The first annual World Hijab Day was celebrated two years prior, in 2013, in recognition of millions of Muslim women who choose to wear the hijab and live a life of modesty. A Bangladeshi American woman who lives in New York, Nazma Khan, came up with the idea to foster religious tolerance and understanding by inviting women (non-Hijabi Muslims/ non-Muslims) to experience the hijab for one day. This annual event invites all women, from all cultural backgrounds, to participate and wear the hijab in support of their Muslim sisters around the world. It is celebrated annually each February 1st.

Once I found out about this holiday, I thought it was a great way to help my community in Rochester understand that the hijab is the headscarf that women from many backgrounds wear, and it's worn for multiple purposes. People, and even some Muslims, misunderstand the purpose of why Muslim women like me wear it. Ever since I moved to America, I realized some people believe that the hijab is a symbol of oppression and segregation, but for me (and many, many others) it is a symbol of modesty. I wanted to dispel the terrorist stereotype and show Americans that the hijab is a proud cultural symbol. World Hijab Day seemed like a perfect way to help educate people and dispel some of the myths.

Two months after starting to attend the World of Inquiry School, I started the World Hijab Day as a way to connect to my classmates and to be included in the community. It was a great time for me as I became introduced at the school and was a way to find similarities with my fellow students in a very human way. I had to write a letter asking my principal for permission to hold the event, and a letter needed to be sent out to all the teachers. I explained to them, "World Hijab Day invites every woman to wear the hijab for a day so they would experience how women who wear the hijab are treated by others. The purpose of this is to educate and feel a part of the school community." My goal was to encourage people to ask questions and not judge others. I asked for the scarves to be donated, and the PTA also donated money for ribbons and carnations for boys and male teachers to show support for the World Hijab Day—I had to take many steps to get there. In the end, over 300 students and teachers in my school wore the hijab.

As we engaged in conversation, one question was pervasive: "Are you forced to wear the hijab?" I was proud to be able to explain to them and say, "Wearing the hijab is your right. When you feel comfortable, you wear the headscarf as a symbol of modesty and the faith within you."

I continued to organize the World Hijab Day at school until I was a senior. So many students and staff supported World Hijab Day that we were featured on the news. World Hijab Day eventually spread throughout the Rochester City School District and beyond. Other schools around the county began contacting me and wanted to follow suit. But there was some backlash as a result of the first World Hijab Day, as well. My ESOL teacher, Kelly LaLonde, and I received death threats and had to be escorted by security to and from school.

I encourage all the immigrant authors in this book and elsewhere to find out what are some of the positive changes they want to see in their communities and start organizing. By organizing World Hijab Day, I wanted to find my way to feel accepted and to raise my voice in support of freedom of religion—one of the cornerstone values in this country. I also wanted to show my community we are more alike than we are different. My activism helped me get recognized. I received the Martin Luther King Jr. Peace Award and Princeton Prize in Race Relations. I also was recognized by the Rochester City School District as the Outstanding Senior for my school. I hope that many authors in this book have taken or will take advantage of many awards and apply (or be nominated).

All the stories in this book, as well as my own, are why I plan on pursuing teaching as my future career. I want to welcome my students—either Americans or immigrants—with open hands, mind, and heart. I will be their guide, just as I was guided by my teachers and school.

Eman Muthana

Founder of the World Hijab Day in Central and Western New York State (Syracuse, Buffalo, and Rochester) and Certified Nursing Assistant living in Rochester, New York

Acknowledgments

The process of creating this book was specifically designed to meet the needs of the young immigrants. Many have had limited or interrupted educations. For these reasons, we recorded the authors telling their stories before we ever approached the written page. Then, in the spirit of the educational and civic engagement opportunities created by our work, we continued the tradition of community engagement by partnering with universities, professors, and students to create community writing and service learning experiences that expand the reach of these stories.

For making this book possible, we have many individuals, organizations, and entities to thank for working tirelessly amid this really unprecedented time.

The most important contributors to this project are the thirty authors who so courageously shared their stories. From hours of preparation in the classroom to bravely telling their stories on camera, from posing for portraits to working with coaches from Brockport TESOL Masters Program and teachers from their local high schools to polish their writing, these young authors have put forth tremendous effort in order to bring you these essays and video narratives. These students are the heart and soul of this work. We are so grateful for and proud of them!

The countries of origin of the student authors vary. Twenty-five student authors originally come from fifteen countries: Albania, Bangladesh, Belarus, Democratic Republic of the Congo (DRC), Greece, Kazakhstan, Myanmar (Burma), Somalia, Sri Lanka, Tanzania, Turkey, Yemen, Honduras, Iraq, Burundi, and Rwanda. Five student authors are from Puerto Rico, an unincorporated territory of the United States. Puerto Ricans are U.S. citizens by birth and colonial migrants, not immigrants. As you will see in their stories, many Puerto Rican students authors are climate refugees.

Rochester City School District Bilingual Language and Literacy Academy, Brighton Middle School (Rochester), Twelve Corners Middle School (Rochester), Lafayette International High School (Buffalo), and Lafayette Newcomer Academy (Buffalo) join with us and share our pride. We would like to thank the principals/directors who lead each of the schools these young authors attend: Teena Jones (Lafayette Newcomer Academy), John Starkey (Lafayette International Community High School), Jim Nuñez (Brighton Twelve Corners Middle School), and Jacqueline Senecal (Bilingual Language and Literacy Academy). Our gratitude is multiplied to our school-site partners.

Two people have been critical to this entire process: Jennifer Raponi in Rochester and Mike Duffy in Buffalo. They have been our on-the-ground advocates working diligently to identify, recruit, coordinate, and prepare the student authors for this project. From working tirelessly with teachers and coaches to ensure the recording was a great success, to polishing student authors' essays and finding community partners, endorsers, and media contacts…without their dedicated commitment this book would not have been possible.

The honor roll of State University of New York (SUNY) Brockport TESOL Master Students and educators in Rochester includes at the top of the list the following individuals: Kristen Hallagan (Brighton Twelve Corners Middle School) and Jill Harris (Bilingual Language and Literacy Academy); and in Buffalo: Kelly Cooper (Lafayette Newcomer Academy), and Michelle Reese and Asma Syed (Lafayette International High School). We also include the coaches in Rochester: Hannah Barone-Crowell, Jaclyn Algier, Lindsay Wiegand and Laura Le; and in Buffalo: Claribel Gonzalez, Michael Duffy, Travis Moore, Michelle Reese, Asma Syed, Clara Mehserle, Melissa Duquette, and Kelly Cooper. These teachers and coaches worked closely with multilingual students throughout the essay development process. Their enthusiasm for this project has not waivered—if anything, it has been strengthened throughout this experience. We are fortunate to have them guiding young people from all walks of life through public education.

In order to accomplish the amount of necessary work remotely from our office and subsequently under the COVID-19 quarantine, the support of key local partners was crucial. We were fortunate to find an incredible partner in Baruch College, City University of New York (CUNY), especially Donna Gitter, a Professor of Law who reached out in August 2019 to establish a partnership with Green Card Voices. Her students from the Macaulay Honors Program, who were studying the history and future of immigration in New York, transcribed the interviewees' stories with care and authored their short biographies. Baruch has been recognized as one of the most diverse colleges in the United States, and these students have a particular appreciation for the immigrant experience. We especially thank these students: Anthony Butta, Yael Carmi, Shirley Chan, Suha Chaudhury, Agnes Chen, Samina Chowdhury, Tasnia Chowdhury, Kyle Climan, Jazmine Freund, Justin Iloulian, Ishraq Kabir, Xin

Lin, Danielle Malpa, Koorosh Nabatian, Aliza Oza, Andreea Pirvulesca, Jairo Reina, Sonel Rubinstein, Jesse Shi, Xinnan Teng, Caleb Varghese, Michelle Wong, and Sara Zinn.

To capture the authors' stories in their own words, GCV Executive Director, Tea Rozman, joined with the production team at Media Active, which was contracted to film the interviews and take the authors' portraits. Media Active is a youth-produced media production studio that provides opportunities for teens and young adults to gain valuable job training and experience by creating professional-quality media products. The beautiful photographs and raw video footage are credited to David Buchanan and Za'Nia Coleman. The latter also edited the incredible video trailer.

We would also like to thank Shiney Her, Graphic Designer, who designed the interior of the book. We thank those who worked with the student authors to transform raw video footage into compelling digital narratives: Asher Dorlester (four videos), Seher Tas (fifteen videos), and Tahiel Jimenez (nine videos).

We thank Zaynab Abdi, GCV Immigrant and Refugee Youth Ambassador, who came to Rochester and Buffalo to meet with each author in this volume to speak about a range of important topics, including her immigrant experience as well as her role both as an author in the first GCV book and as a Malala Fund Delegate. She also traveled to New York City to meet with representatives from The City University of New York to solidify our partnership for this project.

Julie Vang, GCV Program Director, who coordinated and supervised over fifty volunteers (interns, transcribers, coaches, and copy editors) and co-editorial and promotional work throughout the book. Additionally, we extend deep gratitude to Dr. Tea Rozman, whose vision, leadership, and editorial work allowed for the whole project to run smoothly and with a sense of purpose.

Beyond the above mentioned individuals and institutions, we would like to thank the Kennesaw State University English Department that continues to support GCV by providing editorial, research, and writing support. Undergraduate and graduate editorial student interns Joseph Payne, Kristen Roberson, Jooeun Kim, Emmie Sutter, and Ronald Baldwin served as copy editors and produced the glossary under the editorial supervision of Dr. Lara Smith-Sitton. We are grateful to Dr. Lara Smith-Sitton in her role as the department's Director of Community Engagement and for always going above and beyond, including contributing to the editorial work on the essays and other sections of the project.

We thank Karina Boos, Raul Velasquez, and Raul Francisco who helped translate a few authors' interviews from Spanish to English and ensured the accuracy of their words. Special thanks to our foreword author, Eman Muthana, who prefaced these young people's stories with reflections of her own. Thank you to Dr. Veronica Quillien, who designed the study guide *Act4Change* and who is also the lead author of *Voices of Immigrant Storytelling: Teaching Guide for Middle and High Schools.*

Thanks to our funders: individual fund-raisers, funding approved by the past Superintendent of Rochester Terry J. Dade, and major gift donors. Many people and schools also supported us by pre-ordering the book. Without you this publication would not have been possible!

And finally, we thank the GCV Board of Directors for supporting us in bringing this project to New York State. Thanks to all of our board members present: Luis Versalles, Leslie Rapp, George C. Maxwell, Esther Ledesma, Monique Thompkins, Laetitia Mizero Hellerud, Gregory Eagan IV, Debjyoti Dwivedy, Mahlet Aschenaki, Richard Benton, Shukri Hassan, Lara Smith-Sitton, Thorunn Bjarnadottir, and Andrew Gordon; as well as to all of our board members past—Jessica Cordova Kramer, Ruben Hidalgo, Johan Eriksson, Masami Suga, Miguel Ramos, Hibo Abdi, Tara Kennedy, Jane Berg Reidell, Veronica Quillien, Dana Boyle, Katie Murphy-Olsen, Jane Graupman, Ali Alizadeh, Laura Danielson, Jeff Corn, Ruhel Islam, Angela Eifert, Matt Kim, and Kathy Seipp. We are grateful to this team and all others who have helped our mission along the way.

Finally, and most personally, we would like to thank our partners, children, families, and friends for helping each of us put our passion to use for the betterment of society. With the above support, GCV is truly able to realize its mission of using the art of storytelling to build bridges between immigrants and their communities by sharing first-hand immigration stories of foreign-born Americans. Our aim is to help the collective in the U.S. see each "wave of immigrants" as individuals with assets and strengths that make this country remarkable.

Introduction

We are writing these words in precarious times. Images and heartbreak associated with the COVID-19 pandemic, George Floyd's murder in Green Card Voices' hometown of Minneapolis, and the ongoing racial tension and civil unrest brought by the killing of Daniel Prude, an unarmed black man experiencing a mental health crisis at the hands of the police in Rochester, New York.[1] These deaths have affected all of us and laid bare yet again the systemic oppression present in our communities. While we work tirelessly to respond to the immediate needs of our community, we are also committed—more than ever—to continue producing Green Card Voices books. We know that these stories matter deeply...and more than ever in this time. Our publishing work is an important contribution to the much-needed systems-level change, essential change, involving three key processes: thinking, leading, and collaborating systemically. By sharing stories and creating authentic immigrant-centered resources, we hope to pave the way for a more inclusive and supportive society, and in this critical moment, empower these immigrant youth authors and readers alike to address issues of racial inequity and develop deeper racial and cross-cultural understanding.

Historical and Current Considerations

These times have been especially hard because our immigrant communities are already hurting due to the current political and cultural climate, dominant narratives of hate, fear, and xenophobia, which often shape the dialogue surrounding immigration in the U.S. Since 2013, Green Card Voices has been responding to the need for authentic, first-person narratives of America's immigrants and refugees. Our work builds bridges among immigrants and their communities through the art of storytelling. Our organization's programs are designed to foster empathy and promote conversations that provide a foundation for inclusive communities for all by acting as a counterweight to the negative rhetoric and stereotypes about contemporary immigration. Green Card Voices stories remind us that the American landscape and culture are rich due to the mixture of races, ethnicities, and cultures that together create a stronger and more vibrant country.

1. Wilson M., McKinley J, Ferré-Sadurní L., Closson T. and Sarah Maslin Nir (Sept. 4, 2020, updated Oct. 8, 2020). Daniel Prude's Death: Police Silence and Accusations of a Cover-Up. Retrieved from: https://www.nytimes.com/2020/09/04/nyregion/rochester-police-daniel-prude.html

Now, during this time of fear and uncertainty, cases of xenophobia and racism targeting Asian American communities have surged. The COVID-19 pandemic has shown us that even with stay-at-home and quarantine orders, xenophobia lives on, and the need to combat and report xenophobic rhetoric and hate crimes surrounding the COVID-19 pandemic was and will continue to be vital.

We pause here to acknowledge the Native Americans, our original storytellers, whose land we now inhabit. We recognize the descendants of Africans who were forcibly brought here. We remember Frederick Douglass who lived in Rochester, New York, for twenty-five years—this city was his home longer than anywhere else in his life. In his remarkable speech the "Composite Nation", delivered in Boston in 1869, Douglass detailed the importance of equality for all peoples whether White, Black, female, Native American, or Chinese immigrants.[2] We remember the Haudenosaunee (Iroquois), who lived in what is known today as Central New York and Western New York when Europeans first arrived in North America.[3]

According to the United Nations 2019 Immigrant Population Report, 15.4% of our population or 50,661,149 individuals living in this country were not born here.[4] Green Card Voices and our collaborators work every day to lift up stories of these individuals whether immigrants, refugees and, in the case of this particular book, colonial migrants in order for all to be welcomed and made to feel like they belong. We do this through our online video platform, book collections, teaching guides, traveling exhibits, podcast series, and storyteller panels at schools, libraries, and conferences.

Aims of this Book

This book will introduce you to young people living at the crossroads of the immigration debate—young immigrants who live and grow and plan for their futures even as an uncertain political climate and negative immigration rhetoric dominates our media, our politics, and, sometimes, our dinner table conversations. Young authors share their hopes and dreams, which so often include their desires to make the U.S. a better place for all. Their aspi-

2. Douglass, F. (January 28, 2007). 1867 Frederick Douglass Describes the "Composite Nation". Retrieved from: https://www.blackpast.org/african-american-history/speeches-african-american-history/1869-frederick-douglass-describes-composite-nation/
3. Welker, Glenn (Updated July 31, 2020). Iroquois Literature. Retrieved from: https://www.indigenouspeople.net/iroquois.htm
4. United Nations, Department of Economic and Social Affairs, Population Division (August 2019). International Migration Stock 2019. Retrieved from: https://www.un.org/en/development/desa/population/migration/data/estimates2/docs/MigrationStockDocumentation_2019.pdf

rations should remind us of the achievements of earlier immigrants whose significant contributions shaped our country.

Green Card Youth Voices: Immigration Stories from Upstate New York High Schools is Green Card Voices' sixth anthology of essays written by young immigrants. The first book, based in Minneapolis, Minnesota, was published in May 2016 and received a Gold Medal Award from the Moonbeam Children's Book Awards. That collection serves as the template for our success.

We recorded an additional 141 stories from young people in Fargo, North Dakota; St. Paul, Minnesota; Atlanta, Georgia; and Madison and Milwaukee, Wisconsin comprising five additional anthologies from these cities. With *Green Card Youth Voices: Immigration Stories from Upstate New York High Schools*, we travelled to the Northeastern U.S., specifically Rochester and Buffalo, where we worked to share the diverse stories of immigrants and refugees in this region of our country.

New York City is by far the largest city in New York State, followed by cities in its close proximity on Long Island, including Hempstead, Brookhaven, Islip, Oyster Bay, North Hempstead, and Babylon. Outside of those cities, Buffalo is the second largest city in the State of New York with a population of 255,284, followed closely by Rochester with 205,695 residents. Both of these cities have rich and growing immigrant populations.

History of Immigration in Upstate of New York

New York State, according to U.S. Census data, has always been a hub of immigration activity, due in large part to Ellis Island, which was the most heavily used entry point to the U.S. a century ago. Consequently, Rochester and Buffalo have welcomed many different immigrant groups over the years.

After the Revolutionary War and the title to lands in Western New York was obtained from the Iroquois in 1786, New Englanders flocked to all parts of the state. In the two decades after the war, 500,000 new settlers came into New York, and the state tripled in population. Cities along the migration route such as Utica, Syracuse, Rochester, and Buffalo prospered.[5] Large numbers of Irish and Germans came to New York cities in the mid-1800s. New York was the destination for millions of southern and eastern Europeans, especially Italians and Russian Jews, from about 1890 to 1910. The Irish tended to settle in New York City and other large cities, such as Albany, and along

5. The Rochester Central Public Library (2016). Local History and Genealogy. Rochester's Immigrants, Research Guide. Retrieved from: https://roccitylibrary.org/wp-content/uploads/Rochester-Immigrants-Final.pdf

the Erie Canal. Large numbers of Germans settled in New York City, Buffalo, and Rochester.[6]

In 1870, when Rochester's population ranked twenty-second among U.S. cities, 34% of the city's residents were foreign-born.[7] Rochester remained one of the top twenty-five U.S. cities through 1940, when more than 60,000 of its 324,975 residents—or nearly 19%—were born in another country.[8] The turning point for Rochester's population came at the midpoint of the twentieth century. As the number of people living in the city steadily declined, so did immigrants as a share of the population. By 2010, Rochester's population had fallen to 211,977—and the number of foreign-born residents had dropped to 17,281, approximately 8% of the total population.[9]

Following this period, there was a new trend. From 2009 to 2017, the U.S. born population in the city declined by roughly 700, but the foreign-born segment grew by more than 2,000, a 14% increase.[10] This means that as the U.S. born population was leaving the city, immigrants were moving in. Why was this the case? A 2008 policy brief from the University at Buffalo's Regional Institute suggests that "in many aging cities, recent working-class immigrants have helped to reactivate and revitalize gateway neighborhoods, filling housing that might otherwise sit vacant and spurring investment—and making investments themselves—in long-neglected properties."[11] The brief's authors added: "As the region's native population and workforce ages, this young immigrant population will play an important role in filling key employment gaps in, for example, the health care, service and high-tech sectors."[12] As the Upstate New York native population and workforce ages, immigrants at all skill levels will likely play a significant role in the region's economy. In some parts of the upstate region, agencies and private firms have taken steps to attract refugees to stem population decline.[13]

Buffalo, similarly, was a manufacturing center and once the largest grain transshipment port in the world. This was very attractive to immigrants

6. Ibid.
7. Gibson, C. and Jung K. (February, 2006). Historical Census Statistics of the Forign-born Population of the United States: 1850 to 2000. Working Paper No. 81. Retrieved from: https://www.census.gov/content/dam/Census/library/working-papers/2006/demo/POP-twps0081.pdf
8. Smriti, J. (August 22, 2019). Rochester Beacon: Our City of Immigrants. Retrieved from: https://rochesterbeacon.com/2019/08/22/our-city-of-immigrants/
9. Ibid.
10. Ibid.
11. Ibid.
12. Teaman, R.M.: (February 1, 2008). Policy Brief Focuses on Recent Immigration in Upstate New York. University at Buffalo (UB) Regional Institute at State University of New York (SUNY) Buffalo. Retrieved from http://www.buffalo.edu/news/releases/2008/02/9123.html
13. Smriti, J. (August 22, 2019). Rochester Beacon: Our City of Immigrants. Retrieved from: https://rochesterbeacon.com/2019/08/22/our-city-of-immigrants/

looking for jobs with easy access up the Erie Canal. Laid out by the Holland Land Company in 1800, it was first settled mostly by northeastern Americans of English descent. Next came the Germans, the Irish, then Poles, Swedes, Italians, Hungarians, Ukrainians, and Armenians. More recent resettlers include Puerto Ricans, Burmese, Thai, Ethiopians, Sudanese, and Pakistanis.[14] In addition, in 1942 the Bracero Program brought Mexican workers to the States to address the agricultural labor shortage during WWI; this government program brought many Mexicans to New York State.

In 1898, during the Spanish-American War, Puerto Rico was invaded and subsequently became a possession of the United States. The Foraker Act of 1900 established a civil government, ending rule by American generals and the Department of War. A United States Supreme Court ruling, involving the Foraker Act and referring to the island as "the acquired country," soon affirmed that the Constitution of the United States applied within the territory and that any domestic Puerto Rican laws which did not conflict with the United State Constitution could remain in force.[15] The Jones Act of 1917, which made Puerto Ricans U.S. citizens, paved the way for the drafting of Puerto Rico's Constitution and its approval by Congress and Puerto Rican voters in 1952. However, the political status of Puerto Rico, a Commonwealth controlled by the United States, remains an anomaly. In 1948, following the collapse of the once-strong sugarcane industry, Operation Bootstrap allowed Puerto Ricans into the United States to pursue migrant jobs. This government program brought many Puerto Ricans into New York State.

As explained above, while Puerto Ricans are U.S. citizens by birth and colonial migrants: they are not immigrants. Understanding this difference is important in order to have a better understanding of Puerto Ricans' challenges. Their connection to Rochester and Buffalo has much to do with the colonial subordination of Puerto Rico to the United States and the devastating impact of austerity measures imposed by the U.S. government on physical infrastructure and schools. Additionally, the recent refusal of the U.S. government to provide timely and adequate assistance to Puerto Ricans after Hurricane Maria made matters worse.

In recent years, between 2002 to 2015 to be precise, we are seeing

---

14. Saylor, D.L. (2016, January). A Timeline of Immigration in Buffalo. Buffalo Spree. Retrieved from http://www.buffalospree.com/Buffalo-Spree/January-2016/A-city-of-immigrants-then-and-now/

15. Roselló, Pedro Luis Perea (April-June 1963). Santiago, Maria García; Vega, Pedro Malavey; González, José M. Novoa; Goyco, Edwin Toro (eds.). "Res communes omnium". Doctrina. Revista de Derecho Puertorriqueño. Printed in Spain: Imprenta vda. de Daniel Cochs—Cros. 23.—Barcelona (in Spanish). Ponce, Puerto Rico: Pontifical Catholic University of Puerto Rico School of Law. 2 (8): 7–24. ISSN 0034-7930.

significant refugee resettlement into Upstate New York. For example, recent numbers provide the following growth: Burmese: 12,379; Bhutanese: 6,720; Somali: 4,740; and Iraqi: 3,493. According to *A Guide to Community-Based Organizations for Immigrants*, which provides a list of organizations throughout the State of New York, many organizations offer a variety of services such as advocacy, health care, insurance, housing, labor and employment, legal services and lawful status, public assistance, safety, and education. One of those organizations is the International Institute of Buffalo, which was formed in 1910 "to care for the needs of newly arrived immigrant women and girls, and help them assimilate" and continues to remain an active partner in the community.[16] Presently, they welcome, connect and empower the foreign born, and encourage the region's support for different cultures.[17] Similarly, the Office of Bilingual Education and World Languages (OBEWL) is committed to supporting Multilingual Learners/English Language Learners (MLLs/ELLs) and their families across the state. Parents of MLLs/ELLs and former MLLs/ELLs are encouraged to contact the organizations when they need assistance. When families' needs are supported, children have a base to build upon in order to achieve academic success and become college and career ready.[18]

Authors Featured in the Book

For this book we partnered with two high schools in Buffalo—Lafayette Newcomer Academy and Lafayette International Community High School—and two schools in Rochester—Brighton Twelve Corners Middle School and Rochester Central School's Bilingual Language and Literacy Academy. The schools shared similar characteristics, including a high percentage of immigrant students, and as a group, they reflect broader immigration trends in Upstate New York. This approach allows for the reader to gain an understanding of immigrant stories within a state and beyond just those of one city.

As of 2020, Brighton Twelve Corners Middle School in Rochester had nearly 937 students, 3% were English Language Learners and many had successfully reached proficiency during their K–12 school period. While this may seem like a small number compared to the other schools featured in

---

16. Saylor, D.L. (2016, January). A Timeline of Immigration in Buffalo. Buffalo Spree. Retrieved from http://www.buffalospree.com/Buffalo-Spree/January-2016/A-city-of-immigrants-then-and-now/
17. International Institute of Buffalo website (June 2020) Retrieved from https://iibuffalo.org/
18. The New York State Education Department (NYSED), Mid-West Region (2019). A Guide to Community-Based Organizations for Immigrants. Retrieved from http://www.nysed.gov/common/nysed/files/programs/bilingual-ed/mid-west-cbo-list-v7-a.pdf

this book, it should be noted that over a ten-year period of time, the English Learner (EL) population in the Brighton Central School District has more than doubled. Brighton is also unique in its diversity—in 2020, their ELs represented over thirty countries around the world and spoke forty-three different languages.

Bilingual Language and Literacy Academy (BLLA), a Spanish-speaking Newcomer Academy in the Rochester City School District had 120 students in 2019 and 100% of those students were ELs. The majority of students attending BLLA had been displaced from Hurricane Maria: "Nearly 2,300 students displaced from Puerto Rico have entered New York schools since the fall, with 559 of them in Rochester—the most of any district in the state, according to records obtained from the State Education Department."[19] The BLLA was also home to students from the Dominican Republic, Guatemala, Honduras, and Cuba.

In 2019, the Lafayette Newcomer Academy in Buffalo had 260 students—49% of whom were African, 32% of whom were Asian or Pacific Islander, 16% of whom were White/Middle Eastern and 3% of whom were Hispanic/Latino. 100% of students were ELs. Lafayette International Community High School—housed in the same building—had 287 students in 2019: 28% of whom were African, 27% of whom were White/Middle Eastern, 43% of whom were Hispanic/Latino, 21% of whom were Asian or Pacific Islander. Here again, 100% of the students were ELs. The most common languages spoken among students across both schools are Spanish, Arabic, Karen, Burmese, Somali, Nepali, Bengali, and Swahili.

The authors in the Upstate New York book represent such a wide range of experiences and backgrounds. Our authors include new arrivals and graduating seniors, refugees and green card holders. Several were even born in the U.S. but were raised in the countries from which their parents migrated. There are emerging scientists, doctors, business owners, elected officials, and community leaders contained in these pages. And these powerful individuals will shape the Rochester and Buffalo landscapes as well as Upstate New York for the foreseeable future. These young people are wise beyond their years, and their communities will greatly benefit from their shared experiences, talents and insights. There's enough data to show immigrants bring new perspectives, contribute to the economy and encourage all Americans to

19. Spector, J. (March 23, 2018). After Hurricane Maria: Rochester Absorbs More Displaced Students Than Other New York Districts. Democrat and Chronicle. Retrieved from https://www.democratandchronicle.com/story/news/politics/albany/2018/03/23/hurricane-maria-rochester-ny-puerto-rican-students/395305002/

think in different ways, from research to commerce.[20]

Tangible Consequences of National Immigration Policies and the COVID-19 Pandemic

Toward the end of the summer of 2020, just as we were completing the essays for publication, we learned that two of the schools featured in the book—Bilingual Language and Literacy Academy in Rochester and Lafayette Newcomer Academy in Buffalo—closed permanently. Two primary reasons were given for the decision: first, federal policies reducing immigrant resettlement resulted in lower enrollment and second, overall budget concerns—the Rochester City School District was facing a $87 million deficit and to offset this, several programs were discontinued.[21] Impacted students were transferred to new programs and schools beginning in fall 2020.

After the initial shock and the realization that it could be challenging to locate our student authors, we quickly got to tracking down the students from the closed schools. It was hard work, but we were able to locate all of the students, including one young author, Sebastian, who had moved back to Puerto Rico due to the COVID-19 outbreak. We learned that his family felt it was safer there. We are pleased to report that not only did we establish communication with him but also confirmed that he wanted to remain a part of the project.

Significance and Need for this Work

Bravery is what is required to share these stories. This book comes forward in challenging times for immigrants in the U.S. Different segments from the immigrant community face unique challenges. Some of the most noteworthy issues include: the U.S. ban of citizens from eight countries—most of which are majority-Muslim—from entering the U.S.; reduction of refugee admissions to the lowest levels since the creation of the resettlement program in 1980; and relentless and continued attempts to end the Deferred Action for Childhood Arrivals (DACA) program, affecting 800,000 immigrants brought to the U.S. as minor children. Advocates for immigrants say they still haven't found the parents of 545 minors who were separated from

---

20. Smriti, J. (August 22, 2019). Rochester Beacon: Our City of Immigrants. Rochester Beacon. Retrieved from: https://rochesterbeacon.com/2019/08/22/our-city-of-immigrants/
21. Murphy, J. (April 14, 2020). Latest RCSD Budget Proposal Closes Two More Schools, Slashes East Funding. Democrat and Chronicle. Retrieved from https://www.democratandchronicle.com/story/news/education/2020/04/14/rcsd-budget-proposal-closes-two-schools-slashes-east-funding-special-education/2981855001/

their families starting three years ago during President Trump's immigration crackdown at the U.S.–Mexico border.

Now more than ever, Green Card Voices and other organizations that help share the stories of immigrants have roles to play to expand our understanding of the immigrant experience and to highlight the contributions made by this powerful community of individuals. To uphold our country's founding principles of liberty, justice, equality, and dignity for all, we must remember that with diverse newcomers come growth and opportunity.

We hope that this book inspires a spirit of openness and inclusion, which have been the cornerstones of our country. We believe sharing stories is a powerful tool that can help us reach the goal of a fully-integrated and compassionate society. Stories not only empower the teller, whose life experiences and unique contributions become valuable and validated through sharing, but also educate the broader public and help us to see how we all share the experience of being human. These young authors, whose life experiences are unique and whose contributions are so meaningful become valuable and validated through sharing. Through this project we help others "see" and "know" them. We hope you will be as moved as we are by the stories in this book. These writers came to the U.S.—much like generations of immigrants and Americans have before—seeking a place where they could breathe the free air, live life with dignity, and enjoy equal justice under the law. It is our job to build a society of compassion and hope, worthy to be the garden in which their treasured dreams can grow. We believe reading the memories, realities, and hopes will inspire you. Their courage shows that the future of New York—and indeed of the United States of America—is in good hands.

Dr. Tea Rozman

Green Card Voices, Minneapolis, MN

Jennifer Raponi

Mid-West Regional Bilingual Education Resource Network, Rochester, NY

Mike Duffy

West Regional Bilingual Education Resource Network, Buffalo, NY

World Map

Puerto Rico
Green Card Youth Voices storytellers' countries of **birth** (other than US)
Green Card Youth Voices storytellers' countries of **residence or nationality**
Green Card Youth Voices storytellers' countries of **birth and residence/nationality**

Belarus
Kazakhstan
Albania
Greece
Turkey
Iraq
Bangladesh
Myanmar (Burma)
Yemen
Democratic Republic of the Congo
Rwanda
Somalia
Sri Lanka
Kenya
Tanzania
Burundi

Personal Essays

AFRICA
Mogadishu, Somalia

Muna Ismael

Born: Mogadishu, Somalia

Current City: Buffalo, NY

"I REMEMBER WHEN I WAS FIVE YEARS OLD MY MOM USED TO TELL US TO GO UNDER OUR BED AND COVER OUR EARS BECAUSE OF THE GUN."

I was born in Somalia, Mogadishu. I remember when I was five years old my mom used to tell us to go under our bed and cover our ears because of the gun. There were guns everywhere. We didn't leave Somalia. My dad left Somalia to find a better place to live. My dad traveled around and finally find it—a small village in Ethiopia. Then we moved there, but my mom and brother stayed in the capital city of Somaliland in Somalia called Hargeisa. My other siblings and I went back to a small village in Ethiopia called Aw Barre.

When I was eight years old, I came to Ethiopia. I didn't know anyone except one of my dad's friends who lived with her aunt. We stayed with her until we found a house to live in. We found a house that someone used to live in, and we moved to the house. We lived there until we came to the United States. We lived there for four and a half years.

It was good until one day when my dad's friend told us to go to school. My little sister went to a small school, and I went to a big school. I got to wear a uniform, and you have to have books to be in that school, but we didn't have enough money to pay, so I just stayed home until my dad found work. Once my dad found work, I got to go to school. The school was a big school, and it had a lot of people. It was good, but I still didn't understand the language. It was hard for me to learn the language. One day my brother and my mom came to the small village. My brother also started school, but he was above me; he was older than me. He was in fifth grade, and I was in fourth grade.

In Ethiopia, my life was better than living in Somalia. I didn't used to go outside—I just had to stay inside and go under the bed to hide all day. But in the small village we lived in Ethiopia, we had a farm. We shared the farm with my mom's and dad's friend. We had enough food to eat. We planted cabbages, carrots, onions, and other things. We also had a cute animal, a sheep, that used to live with us. The sheep didn't have a name. I also used to go in the woods and collect some trees and make a fire to cook rice and tea in the morning. I used to give my sister some food so she can take to school in the morning. My little sister was born in the small village. My little sister's name is Suad.

In 2012, I found out that we were going to the United States. We didn't know the specific state. Then my brother went to play soccer, and he cracked his leg. He was seventeen years old, so we stayed back in Ethiopia for a few years until he healed his leg. When he healed his leg in 2014, we found out that we're going to the United States. We waited a year, and then on September 25th, 2015 we came to the United States, to Buffalo, New York. We celebrated. We made a lot of food. We even killed the sheep and then made food from the sheep. A lot of people came to celebrate. They brought some clothes and other stuff for us. We packed our stuff—we had a lot of clothes to bring to the U.S.

In my journey on the plane, I didn't know how to speak English. We didn't have other Somalis with us—we were the only Somali people on the plane that took us from Addis Ababa, the capital city of Ethiopia, to New York City. The plane didn't work when we got to New York City, so we stayed for two days. Then we got onto a new plane, and the plane went to Canada then to Buffalo. Nobody waited for us except for the two caseworkers. We were a big family—it was me, my mom, my dad, my two sisters, and my three brothers. One of my sisters came six months before us. She made us food, cleaned the house, and made things for us. We stayed there at the house with her.

There was a big table, and there was a lot of food on it. That was surprising because I didn't know it's going to be there. There were rooms. Our room was already made up, and we just sleep there. We have four rooms, and we can share them. We used to have handmade bed, and here we have some "other stuff-made" beds. In Ethiopia, the bed was stuck on the ground, but here you can move it wherever you want. The walls are different…the houses are different…everything is different.

In my first week in the United States, we went to the hospital because we had to take the flu shot. We met some other Somali and then we did something good—we talked. We speak Somali, and they told us how Buffalo has cold weather. We came in the fall; the leaves on the trees were falling. They told us how Buffalo is cold. You have to wear big boots—shoes—and you have to wear a jacket before you go to school. They told us to wear clothing. In Ethiopia we used to wear something and then go our way.

I started Lafayette High School in eighth grade in 2015. It was hard, but I saw a lot of different people who still didn't speak English, but now they've learned. I stayed in Lafayette for almost five years. I'm now a senior and will graduate. My favorite subject is biology. I like biology because there's more things to learn about human life and generations. I also like English because English is my second language, and I can speak to whoever speaks English. To whoever who doesn't understand, they still can learn English. English is a big language that the world speaks.

I'm a sportsperson. I enjoy playing sports on the weekend. I like basketball, soccer, and volleyball. I enjoy playing basketball with a friend on the weekend. I play every sport in Lafayette. I'm bowling this year, and it's fun playing. It's fun trying new things. With bowling, there are special shoes...special balls even. You just use your hand, and then you play. You throw it, and then you get a point. I'm learning, but I'm doing great! There are teachers who teach bowling. Lafayette teachers are the best.

In my life, I didn't have a lot of friends. I only had one friend, and she became my best friend. Now she lives in Washington. She was my best friend growing up. I met her in Ethiopia, in the village that we used to live in. Her mom was not rich, but we had things to do, and we used to go to the same school. We talked every day. She told me how she wanted to come to Buffalo. We haven't seen each other since 2015. I met a lot of friends in Buffalo, and I have friends now, who are amazing friends. And I have best friends too.

In the future, I want to go to college and study physical therapy. I want to help people. I like that because it is a simple thing. It takes eight years to be a physical therapist, and I just want to be that and help people who live in Somalia. I am looking at college applications. I already got accepted from ECC, Erie Community College, which is in downtown Buffalo, and I'm looking forward to going there. Someday I'm going to Minnesota. I haven't been to Minnesota. I hear there's a lot of Somali there...I like that.... one day I will go.

greencardvoices.org/speakers/Muna-Ismael

ASIA

Nawala,
Sri Lanka

Gunasekera Subasinghe

Born: Nawala, Sri Lanka
Current City: Rochester, NY

"DURING THE DRY SEASON, THERE IS NO RAIN FOR TWO MONTHS. IT'S REALLY HARD... SOMETIMES THE PEOPLE HAVE TO DIG A DEEPER WELL....IF THERE IS NO WATER, WE WOULD HAVE TO GO AND GET IT, AND THAT WAS VERY HARD."

My life in Sri Lanka was pretty good. I lived in the small village of Nawala three hours north of Colombo, the capital. Before coming here my family and friends were pretty happy and good. The schools good. I have one sibling, a brother called S.D. We, as a hobby, played cricket and sometimes played video games. We would also go outside and ride bicycles. Sometimes we traveled with my cousin's family and life was good. I missed my family members a lot.

I like this weather so much here. There are no bugs around here. In Sri Lanka there were so many mosquitos—it was really annoying. There are no snakes here either; in Sri Lanka there are snakes like cobras. One of my dogs died because a cobra killed it. I really like the schools here because there's no fights and no shouting. In Sri Lanka there were fights in the seventh and eighth grade. Also, people get sick a lot in Sri Lanka, and here they do not. So I really like it. When it is the rainy season, there's a lot of mosquitos in Sri Lanka. You get malaria and dengue. Some people die from dengue, so it's really scary.

In Sri Lanka education is bad. I had to ride to school for one hour in each direction—it's really far. The farthest school had better education is why I went there. In my village the schools are really bad, and there are not really good kids. There's a lot of fighting and stuff going on. In school you get hit by teachers if you didn't do your homework, and you get hit if you don't pay attention in class. Sometimes I didn't want to go to school.

I had two dogs and two cats. I also had a parrot that we gave away to a friend. One dog died in an accident. One cat died...an animal ate him, I think because he ran away, and I didn't see him for a few days. There were so many animals around the house—like a forest—a lot of snakes, cobras, wild pigs, cows...and a tiger! It's like a small version of a tiger, and he hates domestic cats.

In the forest there were also big rocks. We climbed the rocks. As we climbed, we saw a porcupine sleeping or monkeys. The monkeys were so annoying—when we were cooking, they would steal our food. We made a fake gun to scare them, but they knew it was fake, so we bought a real one. We showed them or shot to the sky, and they would run away. Behind our house there is a twenty-foot rock. In the stone there was a hole, and we would put sticks in the hole and climb all the way up. I like rock climbing or hiking in really high mountains.

Some of the history of my country starts with the Portuguese. They came, but they went away. Together with the Dutch, Sri Lanka beat the Portuguese. The Dutch tried to take our country, and they fought the British, but then the British took over. They had guns. Before the British came, we didn't know what alcohol was—they gave it to us. In our history there were kings over 2.000 or 3,000 years ago, until 1790—I don't remember the date. Some kings would fight each other, and one king would lose. Then, they would take their valuables like gold and diamonds and hide them underground, under the rocks. Sometimes we go to mountains to see if it's real or not. People predict that they're already taken—maybe it's just rumors. The kings hid and slowly build up their armies. Our last king was very bad. The British killed that king and took our natural resources, like pearls. The British also started planting tea.

Our house in Sri Lanka is at the top of a small hill. We can see the rice paddy fields from there. The farmers would grow rice on the fields, then they would it cut down and store it in their houses. Then, we would have the field to play on—we would play cricket on the rice paddy fields. During the dry season, there is no rain for two months. It's really hard. There is no water in the well either. Some wells do have water, and sometimes the people have to dig a deeper well. We would have to use a "hand pump tube well. If there is no water, we would have to go and get it, and that was very hard.

In 2016, quite unexpectedly and suddenly, my mom won the green card lottery. We didn't expect that to happen, and my family was really shocked. We were able to complete all the paperwork. We had an interview at the embassy, and finally we were able to come here in 2017. Only my mom, dad, brother, and I are in the U.S. The rest of my family members are all in Sri Lanka. My parents miss them a lot because they were so close. The houses were so close together. I think they cried.

When we left Sri Lanka, my extended family came to say goodbye at the airport. After that, we went to the plane and took off. Coming to America was my first time on a plane. When we came, one of my dad's friends was waiting to get us, and I felt so strange and scared. My dad's friends took us to a hotel, and we stayed there two days. My dad's friends helped us—my dad has a lot of friends here. He had a sponsor for the green card. One of my dad's friends is from Pennsylvania, and he is our sponsor. To be a sponsor, you have to have a good job because that's how it works. He's a doctor, I think. We were supposed to stay in Pennsylvania, but we came to Rochester.

When I came here it was summer, so there was no school. The first week we slept a lot because the time difference is nine-and-a-half hours. We were also tired from the journey, so we slept for two days. The first week was strange and different. I never went outside. I was kind of scared because I didn't speak English. We stayed at a hotel the first week until we could find an apartment. My dad and my dad's friend went to find an apartment. They found it in Brighton, and we moved there.

In September I was at first really scared to go to school because I've never been to one here before. All the people were a lot different. I didn't know much English, and so when I went there, I was shaking. Mrs. Halagan helped me a lot. She was able to explain everything to me by using a translating app. She was using Google translate.

The first month in America was not really good. I didn't really speak English in the second month either. I was quiet, but I made some friends. By the third month, it was getting better and better.

I walked the streets a lot with my mom and my brother, but it was cold. Even in the summer! For us the summer here is still cold because in Sri Lanka it was so hot. So we wore jackets, normally we don't wear jackets in the summer; we just wear shorts and t-shirts. We went to the stores and to Lake Ontario. We went fishing. The stores were so different—there are so many little stores in Sri Lanka, more like a market. Some of them are big like Walmart, but they were not as nice as Walmart. There were no air conditioners in stores—only some of the more modern ones. For example, Cargills Food City supermarkets had air conditioners, and their stuff is also more organized, but their stuff is also more expensive. Most of the stores in Sri Lanka are not like this.

I've been here now almost three years. Now I feel better here than in Sri Lanka. In school my favorite subject is math because in Sri Lanka math is really hard. Here seventh grade math is like fifth grade math in Sri Lanka, so math is really easy for me and so is science. The hardest subjects are English, social studies, and health. They involve more English, so it's harder for me. At home as a hobby I play video games, maybe take a walk or work out. Doctor recommended I do some mild workout because I was underweight, so he said gain weight and exercise to get you in better shape. I also like to do wrestling. You have to be kind of tough because you get hit, but rarely you get hurt.

In the future my goal is to be an engineer because my parents told me to be a doctor, but I don't want to be a doctor because I don't like health, science, and stuff. I'm good at computers and that stuff, so I really like computer engineering. I want to stay in the Rochester, New York area in the future.

greencardvoices.org/speakers/Gunasekera-Subasinghe

EUROPE
Gomel,
Belarus

Katsiaryna Liavanava

Born: Gomel, Belarus
Current City: Rochester, NY

"I DIDN'T KNOW HOW SPEAK WITH CHILDREN, AND IT WAS VERY HARD, BUT I LEARN ENGLISH EVERY DAY AND RIGHT NOW IT'S GOOD. I SOMETIMES STILL GET SCARED TO SPEAK ENGLISH WITH OTHER PEOPLE BECAUSE I SOMETIMES DON'T KNOW THE RIGHT WORDS."

I was born in Belarus in 2005, in the city of Gomel, which is the second-largest city in the country located in the southeast. I lived in Belarus for twelve years and went to the school number 53. In the school, I had good friends and good teacher. In Belarus I went to the Arts School for three years. In Belarus they don't have elementary school, middle school, high school like in the U.S.—they have two or three specialty schools. All the grades K-12 are in that one school. Maybe you study for nine grades or eleven grades, and after, you go to university or college.

I very much liked to go to my grandparents' dacha in the summer. We needed to drive thirty minutes to get to it. In this place I like to swim in the river, go for walks with my friends, and help my grandparents around the house. In Belarus, I like to go to the House of Creativity. In this house they have many classes: drawing class, dance class, art class. I go and make bracelets with beads and things made out of paper. In Belarus I go to play piano for several years.

In Belarus I lived with my mother. I'm an only child. My mom wanted to move to another country or another city for better opportunity. My uncle who lived in Rochester told her, "Play green card lottery, maybe you will win the green card." My relatives have lived in Rochester for seventeen years. My mother and I try to apply for a green card. The first year we didn't get a green card. In the second year we won the green card, and we very happy. We filled out the documents and one year later came to U.S. We come to U.S. because there are more opportunities here.

I still remember how I found out that I was moving to the U.S. On that day my mom went to work. At work my mom called me and said she won the green card lottery. She was very happy. She bought a cake and came home after work and said to me, “We won the green card!” It was not very hard to leave my home, but it was hard to leave my family—my grandparents, my dad, uncle, and my friends at school. I still talk to my friends in Belarus. I sometimes put American things in a box and send it to my friends and grandparents in Belarus.

On the day of our big journey, my mom and me left in the morning. My grandparents drove me and my mom to airport in another city called Minsk. My granddad drove three hours. This was my first time flying in an airplane. This was my dream, and my dream came true. We flew from Minsk, Belarus to Moscow, Russia, and then from Moscow to New York City, New York, and after that from New York City, New York to Rochester, New York. Flying took about twenty hours in total with many stops.

When we got to Rochester airport, we very tired. The time difference is eight hours, so I was very tired because of that as well. My relative took us to his house. The next day, my relative say we will go to the museum. This museum was huge and beautiful. It’s called The Strong National Museum of Play. I really liked it. On this day I also went to the school to meet my teachers. In this day, they gave me a locker and password. I tried to open it ten times, but I couldn’t open it. After ten times, I opened it, and I very happy.

Five days after coming to U.S. I started school. I got up at 6:00 a.m. in the morning and got ready to go to school. In Belarus I wake up at 7:45 a.m. to go to school, and it only took ten minutes, but in U.S., my mom took me to the bus stop and the school bus took me to the high school, but I need to go to the middle school. When I arrived, I looked around and it did not look like my school building. I was very scared on the bus. I did not know how to ask “Can I sit here? Where is my school?” Eventually I followed the students to the middle school. I went to the auditorium and waited twenty minutes, then students started to go to classes. I did not know how to get to my homeroom; I only knew one teacher. Soon other teachers helped me find my classes, and I took my schedule to ask for help.

I had two big books, and I was carrying the big books everywhere. The books were for Chemistry and Social Studies. I did not have a big backpack at first, so I had to carry the books everywhere in my arms. I needed help with my locker because I couldn’t find it. I asked a girl for help. It was hard to open. My first day my schedule was wrong. My music class and lunch class were switched, and the teacher helped me to get it fixed. On this day I met my teacher and my new friends. There were two boys in my homeroom who spoke

Russian and that was helpful.

The teacher asked me to write my last name, but I didn't know how. In Belarus, we write in Cyrillic, and I still needed to learn how to write in English. The school itself is very confusing too. There are two gym classes and four gym teachers. I didn't understand when the teacher called my name because it was hard for her to pronounce it. After everyone was called, I showed her my name on my schedule, and she said, "Oh, I called you." She helped me get a locker for gym class, and it was hard to open. A girl helped me open it for a week then I learned how to.

The second week was very nice. I went to school; I tried to do my homework and use Google translator to help me. My friend Stivia helped me with my homework. I met her on the second day of school. She is from Albania and has been here for two or three years. She knows where classes are in the building, so she helped me find my classes. I asked with a Google translator what her phone number is and sometimes send her a message to help me with my homework. My first very good friend was Stivia.

This same week, my mom and I went to look at a new apartment for us to live in. We also bought stuff for our new home. One month after coming to the U.S., things were very good. I was able to study English and my mom was able to look for a new job.

At first, I did not understand a lot of information, but I understand a little bit now. It's was very hard to study English because I didn't know how to speak it—I didn't know one word. I didn't know how speak with children, and it was very hard, but I learn English every day and right now it's good. I sometimes still get scared to speak English with other people because I sometimes don't know the right words. Now I'm middle school, in eighth grade. I study in a school where the students and teachers are wonderful. My favorite teachers are Ms. Hallagan and Ms. Martinez. I have many friends at school, and everyone is nice to me. My favorite class is art because I like to work with my hands. I like to learn how to draw and make cups out of clay with flowers on it.

Outside of school I like to paint my nails and cook. I like to watch movies in English. I really like it and it's very cool. On the weekend, I like to go to the shop and go shopping with my mom. I like to call my grandparents in Belarus. I really like living in the U.S. My mother went back to school too. She is studying in Monroe Community College and wants to be a dental hygienist in the future. As for me, in the future I want to finish school and go to college. I would like to get a job in the arts. I want to maybe draw pictures for businesses.

Next year I think I will go to visit Belarus. This will be my first visit back in Belarus. When I go to Belarus in the summer, I will go see my school and my favorite teacher. Maybe give her something from America and see what has changed and go for walks with my friends. I look forward to seeing my grandparents, go to their country house, and swim in the river, maybe go to the House of Creativity again.

greencardvoices.org/speakers/Katsiaryna-Liavanava

NORTH AMERICA
San Juan,
Puerto Rico

Bryant Pagan

Born: Greenwood County, South Carolina

Raised: San Juan, Puerto Rico

Current City: Buffalo, NY

"ON SEPTEMBER 16, 2017, HURRICANE MARIA HIT PUERTO RICO....THE SOUND OF THE WIND MADE ME FEEL SO SCARED—THE WINDOWS WERE SHAKING, AND THERE WERE OTHER SOUNDS LIKE METAL HITTING METAL....ONCE IT STOPPED RAINING, WE WENT AROUND THE NEIGHBORHOOD. EVERYTHING WAS PRETTY MUCH DESTROYED."

My biological dad is originally from Guatemala, My mom is from Mexico. I know my mom's name is Maria. I have a biological sister, and I think she is 20 years old, but I don't know her. I was told that I was born in South Carolina and adopted by a couple from Puerto Rico four days after I was born.

I lived in the United States in the state of South Carolina for two years. When I was two, we moved to Puerto Rico. So most of my life, I lived in Puerto Rico. My adopted mom's name is Leviani Torres, and my adopted dad's name is Enrique Pagan. They are so good, and I love them so much because they do everything for me. When I moved to Puerto Rico, I was their little baby. I remember that we used to live in a small house, but my dad and mom worked hard to make it bigger and bigger. I remember my friends when I started attending the Head Start program. I was three or four years old. I used to fight with another kid every day. I still remember him. Then, I moved to another Head Start school closer to the place I was living. There I made a lot of friends.

During my first-grade education, I was able to learn how to read and write. Then I went to second grade. I really liked it in second grade because I learned the multiplication table and division. Even though I felt that it was too much stuff to learn for me, I really enjoyed it. The sixth grade was a good grade because I made a lot more friends, and I was still receiving good grades.

Then, the first two months into my seven grade, September 16, 2017, Hurricane Maria hit Puerto Rico. I was really scared because it was my first time experiencing a hurricane. Around 1:00 a.m. the electricity went out. I was so scared because I don't like to be in the dark. I didn't want to sleep by myself in the room, so I moved to my parents' room. I was sleeping in a small bed that we managed to fit in my parents' bedroom. The sound of the wind made me feel so scared—the windows were shaking, and there were other sounds like metal hitting metal. During the first night, every time I would wake up my parents would tell me, "Go back to sleep." I would fall back asleep and then when I woke up around 5:00 a.m., I looked outside through the window, and I couldn't see because it was so dark, but, somehow, I was able to see trees lying in the streets and water running from all directions. Since there was no electricity, it started to feel very hot, and I also started thinking about all the electrical appliances, like refrigerator. Suddenly, within minutes it started raining very hard. I just kept looking through the window to see outside, but it was hard to see anything at all.

During Hurricane Maria things were bad, and we had a lot of rain. At around 10:00 a.m. I woke up again; it had been raining for a long time. My mom opened the front door just to see what was surrounding our house. The wind was so strong that it pushed us back inside the house, and we had a hard time closing the door back again. Because of this, we stayed inside the house during the entire hurricane. We just kept hoping that it would end soon.

Once it stopped raining, we went around the neighborhood. Everything was pretty much destroyed. Even the pavement of the street was cracked. I was shocked when I saw a lot of the electrical poles broken and lying down on the ground with pieces of power lines scattered all over the place. We had to stay at home for two weeks. At least we had running water. There were some areas in much worse condition—they stayed without electricity and water for a much longer period. Their situation was so bad that it turned into a real humanitarian crisis.

When the two weeks passed, we decided to go visit a close relative that lived in another city. Their conditions were pretty much the same as ours. The strong winds had blown away the roof of their house. We then went to visit my brother in the city of Ponce. When we arrived at his place, we realized that there was nobody at this house. We didn't know where he and his family had gone. Because the cell phone network didn't work, we couldn't communicate, so it was hard to get a hold of them.

In my hometown, the downtown area is one of the most visited areas of the city. Everyone likes to go downtown with family and friends and spend time together. There were a lot of good places to go eat and shop, and there were so many great recreational parks. The downtown was completely destroyed. Buildings were damaged with broken windows. The pavement of the main street was cracked due to the strong force of the water that flowed through the streets.

Weeks after the hurricane I began to play outside with the kids from the neighborhood. We were still unable to do much, but every day around 5:00 p.m. we would go to the balcony and sit there for a while. We would sit in complete silence for a minute or two and just look at everything around us. Our phones weren't working due to the poor signal, but we used our phones for other things. Luckily, we were able to charge them in our dad's car.

One day my parents told me that they were planning to move to the U.S. That same day we started packing all our stuff, and my mom withdrew me from school. My mom and I left on November 13, 2017, almost two months after Hurricane Maria hit. My dad decided to stay in Puerto Rico for a while to finish selling some household items. At that time, we didn't know for how long we would stay in the U.S. On the day we left, I was so scared because it was my first time on an airplane. My dad took us to the airport in Ponce, Puerto Rico. He hugged me. I felt so sad. We checked-in our bags. I thought it was cool how they scan the bags. We went through TSA and then just waited for an hour in the lobby area to board the airplane.

When we boarded the airplane and sat on the seats, I kept looking through the window. The airplane took off, and I started feeling all these emotions. I felt that my body wanted to go down as the airplane was lifting. My mom told me no to worry about it. She said that it was kind of normal to feel that way until you get used to it. It was a few hours of travel time until we landed in the U.S. When we have arrived in the U.S., we were able to use our phones for the first time in two months. But since there was still no signal in Puerto Rico, we couldn't even tell our family that we were flying to the U.S. from Puerto Rico because of Hurricane Maria. The city where we landed was not our final destination. My mom called my sister to let her know that we have arrived and were planning to stay at her place in Buffalo, New York. She was happy to hear from us.

From there we boarded an airplane for the next flight. I didn't feel anxious because I knew that there was somebody waiting for us after the short flight. When we landed in Buffalo and were reunited with my sister. She had visited Puerto Rico several months before Hurricane Maria. I was very happy because it was the first time seeing my little niece—she was still a baby. We went straight to my sister's house. On the second day in Buffalo, they enrolled me in the school.

On the first day of school I was so scared, and I felt very uncomfortable due to my English language skills. I was happy that it was a bilingual school and that my teachers supported me. It was a big school, so different than in Puerto Rico. My classroom was on the third floor. My teacher introduced me to a student named Luis, and she asked Luis to help me. It was very funny because everyone thought that I was a girl because my hair was very long. I made a lot of friends, and I started to learn English. I assimilated to the new environment and new culture. I really felt the difference between the U.S. and Puerto Rico during the lunch break. I was so used to playing outside after eating my food, in the U.S. this was not the case.

Several months after I started school in Buffalo, I entered a time where I felt a lot of rebellion. I was misbehaving in class and just not really trying my best. I was still doing my work at school, but I was always talking a lot during class. The teacher would call my name several times and tell me to stay quiet when she was talking and presenting. I started getting bad grades, until one day when my teacher decided to call my mom making her aware of my behavior in class. My mom had a conversation with me, and she told me that my only responsibility was to get good grades in class. I told my mom that I would change my behavior and that I would give it my best at school.

Several days later, my dad and my brother and my brother's family all arrived in the U.S. They came to Buffalo, New York too. I did not see my father for about four months. After his arrival, my parents decided to look for a new place to live because my mom felt that it was important to have our own home. We appreciated my sister's help and support during this difficult situation, but we didn't want to take away her own space and privacy. I was very happy because the family was reunited. As a matter of fact, I also started getting better grades at school.

After six months of my parents looking for an affordable place to live, I started to notice that they were getting a little anxious to move back to Puerto Rico. Because my parents could not find an apartment for us, we decided to return to Puerto Rico. Before we returned, there was a school trip and we went to Washington, DC for three days. I had such a great time with my classmates. We went to the White House; we went to some of the most visited places in DC. We went to a lot of museums, and we ate a lot of pizza.

Two weeks after the trip, we sent a lot of the stuff to Puerto Rico. The day we left the U.S. everybody was sad because we were leaving. My dad had already left for Puerto Rico by that point. He wanted to have the house ready for us with everything set up, and my mom and I stayed back so that I could finish the school year. One day after school, when I got to my house, my mom had everything packed up and ready for us to leave. We had one connecting flight to get to Puerto Rico from Buffalo, New York. I remember we landed in an airport where there were a lot of Puerto Ricans boarding the airplane. We landed in the city of Ponce in Puerto Rico. There was still a lot of reconstruction going on, but I had a good feeling being back at home.

When I started eighth grade, I was able to reunite with my old friends. They were happy to see me back, but they were telling me that I looked different because I had cut my hair—now my hair was short. During the school year, I thought about my friends in the U.S. When the school year of eighth grade ended, and my friends and I had a graduation ceremony. I received an award of academic excellence. I also received several other medals for academic achievement. It was an exciting moment to receive the awards and be recognized for academic performance, but I would still think about the U.S. I would ask myself how things would be if I went back to U.S.

During the summertime, I would just stay at home and play video games with two of my best friends, but two weeks before the start date of the new school year, I noticed that my dad had built a sign that said "For Lease" with his contact information. My initial thought was that he wanted to rent one of the rooms in our house, so I never asked him anything about it. I was also noticing things being different around the house. Then one day, I told my mom that I needed to reorganize my room before school started, but she had a surprised reaction. I asked if they were planning to move back to the U.S., and they said, "yes." I had mixed emotions. I felt sad and scared at the same time. I was also just really upset and sad, but then happy too…all of these emotions at the same time.

This time all three of us left Puerto Rico together and headed to the U.S. for the second time, but we had challenges. The flight was canceled due to bad weather, and we were rerouted to Newark, New Jersey. We had to get new boarding passes and had already been waiting in line for four hours when I realized it was already 1:00 a.m. I felt so tired. I slept on a chair and did not wake up until 8:00 a.m. the next day, but my mom was still waiting in line. They finally changed our boarding passes so that we could fly to Buffalo, New York. When we got to the gate, I noticed that they were calling people's names before letting anyone board the airplane. Everyone was saying, "Wait to get your name called." At that point, my parents told me that they had already changed the flight to a new date, so now the departure day was Saturday—that day was Thursday. So, we spent two days at the airport. We received a voucher for food, but that was not enough to afford food because of the high airport food prices.

After all that ordeal, we finally landed in Buffalo once again and we were reunited with the rest of the family. We had not seen them for a year, so it was good to see them. I started ninth grade in a new school, Lafayette High School. Lafayette is a bigger school with a very diverse population of students. I started to make new friends and Luis, my friend from seventh grade was there too. My family stayed with my sister for five months. We also spent time with my brother and his family. Just this past month, we finally got our own place. My dad bought the furniture for the new apartment, and we moved all our belongings to the new place. I feel that we are finally settled now.

I really want to become someone in life. I feel that will be a gift to my parents as they will be paid back for all the efforts they have made for me. I would like to surpass my limits and become someone in life who is able to show my parents how much I appreciate them. Although I miss my island, I am happy to be in Buffalo. I am excited to see what the future brings.

greencardvoices.org/speakers/Bryant-Pagan

ASIA
Basra,
Iraq

Zainab

Born: Basra, Iraq
Current City: Buffalo, NY

"MY DREAM IS TO BECOME A DOCTOR AND GO BACK TO IRAQ AND HELP PEOPLE THERE."

I moved out of Basra when I was six years old. There was a war between Shias and Sunnis in Basra. That's when I lost my father. We went to Jordan with a car and then we were having the same problem because they were burning Shia people's houses. In Jordan, they would judge me because I am a Shia. I had a lot of fights because of that so after two years and a half, my family said that we were going to the U.S. I was shocked because I did not want to go.

In Basra, all I remember was staying home because I was little—I was around five or six. My brothers and my dad used to get out of the house only because there were some people who were taking children from houses. A lot of people passed away, and we saw their bodies. We didn't see my dad's dead body, so I don't believe he is dead.

I lived in Jordan for two and a half years with my seven brothers. I am the youngest. It was a hard life. I remember my mom always went to the hospital for surgeries, and they were doing it wrong for her. They weren't good doctors. There was no war, but they hated Shia, so that's what makes them burn Shia houses.

One day my mom told me that I was going to go to the U.S. I was shocked by it. I still wanted to go back to Iraq. We went from Amman, Jordan and flew straight to Buffalo. When I came to Buffalo, I saw my house and my uncle. It was a confusing journey. I didn't feel nothing different when I first came to Buffalo. The only thing I was doing was staying at home and loudly crying the whole day because I wanted to go back. I wasn't alive here. It wasn't any different than Basra or Jordan because I stayed at home all the time.

Then two or three weeks later, I went to school. I went to school at six grade. I was having a hard time figuring out how to speak English, but I had a teacher there—she was Arabic. She helped me a lot. I started going out and figured out how America is. I had heard a lot of about it. I went out, and I learned how to speak English. I have cousins living here who were born in the U.S., and they helped me. It was weird because my cousins don't speak much Arabic, which is all I speak. It was confusing to figure out how to talk to them because they don't know much. After I finished sixth grade, I came to Lafayette International, and I've been here for three years. My favorite subject is global, U.S. history, and math. I find it interesting. I find math hard and confusing, but that's what I like about it. I like global and U.S. history because I like what happened in the past, even if it was wars, I like to know what happened.

Afterschool and on the weekends, sometimes I go out and sometimes stay at home. I went out of the house to see Niagara Falls, New York City, and visit Michigan. I like to see big buildings because I haven't seen them before. I went to Times Square and a place named Brooklyn. I went to Michigan with my mom and my brothers to visit my cousins. I went to halal restaurants and saw many Arab speaking people.

In the future, I want to go back to my country. My dream is to become a doctor and go back to Iraq and help people there.

greencardvoices.org/speakers/Zainab

ASIA
Almaty,
Kazakhstan

Alex Tsipenyuk

Born: Almaty, Kazakhstan
Current City: Rochester, NY

"ALL THE STUDENTS IN MY CLASS WERE ALL COMPLETELY DIFFERENT FROM THE PEOPLE THAT I USED TO BE IN CLASS WITH. THEY WERE INTERESTED IN WHERE I WAS FROM, BUT I COULDN'T SPEAK WITH THEM, AND I COULDN'T MAKE FRIENDS."

My life in Almaty wasn't bad. I had a friendly family. I had a lot of friends. I lived in a big city, Almaty—the largest city in Kazakhstan with a population of two million people. I had everything that I needed. My family wasn't poor but wasn't rich. My mom says that we were like in the middle class, but I still think that we were little higher than middle class.

I used to hang out with my friends almost every day from the morning until the evening until fifth grade when we all got computers, phones, and stuff. Then, we started to stay home more and not go outside as much. I didn't like school much and still don't, but it was boring sometimes but my friends made it fun too. I had hobbies—I used to play soccer all the time, but then I just got tired of it, so I stopped. During the winter, we used to go to the ice rink to go ice skating and play hockey. We played hockey all the time during winter. When I first got to America, the weather reminded me of Almaty with the wind blowing in my face. There's not that much snow in Rochester but there, in Almaty, there was a lot of snow.

Before we applied for the green card, my aunt and uncle, who were already living in America, were calling every week and talking about life here. My dad admired it. My mom and dad both applied for the green card lottery. If my memory serves me, it was September or October of 2015 when my mom told me that we won the first part of the lottery, but there were two parts. We had to pass the interview, which was the second part. In December 2015 or January 2016, we went to have the interview with the American Consular Officer at the U.S. Embassy. We went all together as a family. They asked us what we would want to do if we moved, as well as some other things. We passed the interview! And our way to America was open.

We had half a year or a year to move to America. My mom said that I still needed to finish fifth grade in school. Once I finished it, we were planning to move. It was very hard to say goodbye to my friends and relatives—it was pretty challenging. They were upset that I was leaving, not because I got the lottery. I remember the day we went to the soccer field. It was 9:00 p.m. and I said, "Ok guys, goodbye, I'm leaving."

When we moved to America, it was just me, my mom, my dad, and my brother who came. Our dog, who is also part of the family also came. She is an English Spaniel, and her name is Sima. She's almost twelve years now, I have had her since I was three. She's an amazing dog—like really amazing—she's very friendly. She never bites. She's very nice.

There are definitely things that I miss. First of all, I had to give up my friends. Then, Kazakh food and the Kazakh culture and mentality in general. Kazakhs are very hospitable, and so are Americans, but it's just different. The people in general are so different. When I came here, I was surprised about a lot of things. I was walking in the street and people were smiling at me. I was like "Why? Why are you doing this? I don't even know you." But then I realized that everyone, almost everyone, does that. Some of the food I miss is shashlik, which is a meat, lamb or pork, that is skewered and grilled. It could be chicken also, but then it's not shashlik. I also miss beshbarmak, which is Kazak food; it's made of dough and meat also.

My first day in the United States I was very excited, but at the same time I was a little scared because of new country, new language, new school, new people. I think my mom and dad were scared more than me because they're old and they had to take responsibility. They took care of me and my brother and my dog. They had to find a job, and I think it was very challenging for them. For the first couple of months they were cleaning, and then later found new jobs, better jobs. I came during summer. It was June 18th, and the first two months were okay…they were good. We traveled around the city. My other relatives from my dad's side showed me different places…they showed me my school. My mom and dad saved money from Kazakhstan and used that money to buy everything. My aunt and grandma had been in the area for twenty years and helped with everything. The summer was good.

When the school started after the first few months here, it was the worst time in America because I didn't know the language. I couldn't speak it, and I couldn't understand it. All the students in my class were all completely different from the people that I used to be in class with. They were interested in where I was from, but I couldn't speak with them, and I couldn't make friends.

I didn't understand what they were saying. I liked the school here because the teachers are very nice. They don't scream at you because maybe you didn't do your homework, or you forgot to bring something. They were okay with it. In Kazakhstan the teachers usually screamed when they don't like something, or they don't like you. They kick you out in the hallway if you don't behave. In the U.S., they always give you an opportunity to fix your grades, and this is very nice.

Now I'm in tenth grade; I'm a sophomore. I don't really have any hobbies—I just like to come home from school and relax. Because my dog is getting older, she doesn't want to play anymore. My current life is pretty good. It's definitely much better than it was the first year, but I cannot say it's much better than in my country. It's like the same, but the standard of living in the United States is higher than in Kazakhstan. Everyone in America, well most people, have property and have houses. We used to live in apartment. The places were not as good as here.

In school my favorite subjects are sciences, but I really don't like math, especially geometry, where you have to prove that the square is rhombus. I think this is kind of silly. I like biochemistry because it's more interesting. In the future, I really hope I can contribute to the U.S. in a scientific way, maybe invent a cure for cancer or other disease or create a substance that lets you eat, and you don't get fat. I love eating. I think it's one of the best things in the world.

I can say that the United States is a country of opportunities and if you are poor you can become rich, but you have to work for it. I think this is why millions of people want to come here. We are very happy that we are here.

greencardvoices.org/speakers/Alex-Tsipenyuk

AFRICA
Uvira,
Democratic
Republic
of the Congo

Immaculee Mukeshimana

Born: Uvira, Democratic Republic of the Congo

Raised: Bwagiriza Refugee Camp, Burundi

Current City: Buffalo, NY

"IN BURUNDI, I WENT TO SCHOOL IN THE AFTERNOON, NOT IN THE MORNING. HERE, I CAN COME TO SCHOOL WITH PANTS, BUT IN BURUNDI YOU HAVE TO WEAR A LONG DRESS. THERE WERE MANY DIFFERENCES. IN BURUNDI, THEY TEACH US IN FRENCH. HERE, IT'S ENGLISH."

My mom and my dad told me that in Congo there was too much war. There was fighting almost every day. Before they moved to Burundi, they shot and bombed our house. They told me that I was a baby, and they shot everybody. Even now, my mom still has the shrapnel scars everywhere. Our house was bombed when everybody was inside, so we decided to move.

I remember many things about Burundi, but I don't remember many things about Congo because I left Congo when I was three months old. I left our country because of war. I lived in the Bwagiriza Refugee Camp for 17 years. I had a hard time in Burundi because I did not have enough food to eat. I didn't have many things, like water and medicines. I remember the people in Burundi. I remember my friends in Burundi. Many people didn't like refugees.

I went to kindergarten in Burundi. School was not that bad, and it was also not that good. It was good because we had teachers from Congo. They taught us about Congo. We had a good teacher, but we didn't have books. The teacher didn't have books to read or a computer or anyway to look at the news, so they teach us the things that they know. In the morning, the middle schoolers go to school. In the afternoon, the high schoolers go to school. When I was in high school, I went to the school in the afternoon. I was always late to school because I had to search for water. We didn't have water, so we had to go find water. Everyday I was late.

On the weekends when we didn't have school, I would usually go to church. I was a singer and I would go to practice. At night, when the sun goes away, we sleep to be safe. If you are outside at like 7:30 or 8:00 p.m. and the police see you, they will take you to jail. When the sun goes away, everybody should be in the house to be safe.

One day, they told us that we had to go to start the resettlement process. I was so happy that day. I felt like, "Oh my God, this is not true." I was like, "Is it true or they are just lying to me?" But on August 2nd, 2016, we went to the Refugee Center, when we finished, they said that no more refugees could come to America because President Trump said that they don't want any more refugees. I was so sad. I was thinking before I heard that how my life is going to change because I'm going to have a school, a good school, a better education. Then they said that Trump said, "No." I feel so bad. I did not go to school for two days because I was not feeling good. Then, one year later, they said that he said, "Yes, you guys can continue the process to come to America."

We had interviews in the refugee camp. Then they gave us the date to go into the city of Bujumbura. So my family—my mom, dad, and siblings—we used a car to go to Bujumbura to see the doctor, but after seeing the doctor, my dad died. So then they told us again that my family could not go to America because one person was gone from our family. We said it was okay, and we stayed in Burundi. About three months later though, they said that we could come to America.

When we started to try to come again, I was with my mom and my five siblings. I have three brothers and two sisters. My great-grandmother and grandmother also lived in the same camp but when we went to Bujumbura to interview, they stayed in the camp. My family went to Bujumbura in December to start the immigration process and medical check. My great-grandmother and grandmother went later in March to Bujumbura to start the immigration process and get their medical check. We all got to go but not the same day.

I remembered that day when we left for the U.S. We went to airports in Bujumbura and Ethiopia, then went to Washington, DC and to Buffalo. I was so scared because it was my first time sitting in an airplane, and I was going to be with people I did not know. I was also so happy because I knew I was going to see my cousin who had lived in the United States for four years. When we got there, my cousins, my uncles, our friends, and our case workers were waiting for us. It was in the summer. The first day, I stayed with my cousin. It was night when I got there. It was 8:00 p.m. and I was afraid that the police would take us to jail. They said, "No, in America, you can walk outside as long as you like. If you want to, you can stay out all night." But I was scared, I asked them, "Are you okay to walk outside at 8:00 p.m.?" Again they said, "It's okay, you can go outside as long as you like." It was 8:00 p.m. and the sun was still out. They showed me many things when I got there. The first week, they took me to Niagara Falls. Every night they took me out and they showed me the town, the village. They showed me the park downtown.

After three weeks, I went to summer school. It wasn't actually like school because it was mostly two people teaching us English. My siblings and I were in the same class. It was different here because in the United States, I go to school in the morning. In Burundi, I went to school in the afternoon, not in the morning. Here, I can come to school with pants, but in Burundi you have to wear a long dress. There were many differences. In Burundi, they teach us in French. Here, it's English. We can change class-to-class here, but in Burundi you have to stay in the same class and the teachers change from class-to-class. In Burundi, there is no lunch for the students and every day we had to learn ten lessons. It is so different here.

In Burundi, we used to eat the same food every day. They gave us only beans and fufu for one month. We had to eat that food every day. But here, you can change the food you eat at dinner and lunch. In Burundi, it's the same food for breakfast, lunch, and dinner. In Burundi, we didn't have enough water or enough food. But here we have enough food and water. In Burundi, if you are sick and have money you can go outside the camp and get medicine. But if you are in the camp and don't have money then you get the same medicine, no matter what your sickness. They gave everyone the same medicine. They gave medicine in blue cups or pink cups, but it was the same medicine just in different cups.

My culture is different in Burundi than it is here. When I was born in Congo, I lived with my family—everyone, including my uncles. But here, it's just us and some of my cousins, not the whole family together. We would speak our home language when we are at home, but here I have to learn English and other languages. Our culture also changed because we are four families together here. We are together and a part of the American culture now.

I've been in the United States since June 12, 2018. This year, 2020, many things are good. When I came, I wasn't speaking English—only "yes" and "yeah." Now, I can speak English. I can go to school. Now, I'm in the tenth grade. I like all the subjects, but math is a little bit confusing to me. I like science and biology, because it's easy for me. I feel like it is not complicated, and I choose to be a doctor because biology is easy for me. I like to stay after school for Global Studies class, but I don't because our teacher for Global never stays after school, so when I have homework or anything, I do them in Advisory class. My siblings also go to school. They are in the ninth, seven, six, fourth, and second grades. My mom found a job. She works at night. My big sister also lives in New York State but near Syracuse. She lives in another city because of her school. She is older and couldn't go to public school, so she goes to Job Corps.

When we came to the United States, we came separately from my great-grandma. We came in June and she came in July. She lives in Buffalo now. She was 111 years old when she came to Buffalo, and now she is 113 years old. Before COVID-19, I would see my great-grandma almost every day—at least three to five days each week. When I visit her, she'd tell me the story about my country and the life before and after independence. She says after independence there was more freedom, people can do what they want. We are the tribe of Banyamulenge. Some people said they wanted our tribe to leave, and they don't want us to be considered Congolese. Now, since we are at home during COVID-19, we talk on the phone, and it is difficult to talk to her on the phone. My great-grandma thinks phone calls are from her grandchildren in Burundi, and it makes her cry. My grandmother lives with my great-grandmother, I have a good relationship with both. Sometimes when they tell stories, the other says, "You don't know, it happened like this."

My goal is that I want to finish my school in five years. After I finish school, I want to be a doctor. I want to be a doctor because I love science so much, and I know science. I do very well in science and being a doctor is about science. I want to help people that are sick. I also think about working in a pharmacy because when you work in the pharmacy, you do not have to be on call.

greencardvoices.org/speakers/Immaculee-Mukeshimana

ASIA
Lüleburgaz,
Kirklareli,
Turkey

Ayşe

Born: Lüleburgaz, Turkey
Current City: Rochester, NY

"I THINK THE MAIN THING IS THAT YOU GIVE UP SOME OF YOUR CULTURE AND YOUR LANGUAGE AT A CERTAIN POINT IN THE AMERICAN SCHOOL. BECAUSE YOU CAN'T UNDERSTAND, IN ORDER TO UNDERSTAND, YOU HAVE TO TAKE ON THEIR LENSES AND PERSPECTIVE TO ADAPT."

I was born in Lüleburgaz, Turkey in my grandparents' house. I didn't live there for long, but I still have memories from there from time with my older brother. Right under my grandparents' house there was a market, and I would always go there with my friend to buy some snacks like Çubuk kraker or tutku or ice cream.

I grew up all over Turkey. I always moved because of my dad's job. My dad was a university professor. I eventually moved to Ankara, the capital. I had a really big house and it was really beautiful. My house was in a really large and warm neighborhood that I lived in. Right next to my house, there was a picnic area that I would always go to with my family at night. I also had a large group of friends, and we would always go back to a really big garage and play hide and seek. In Ankara, I was in a private school because my dad was able to afford it at that time.

We thought we would stay in Ankara for a really long time. But then the political administration of Turkey was really getting worse, and my dad didn't really like the atmosphere. He wanted to go away for about two years. That is why he partnered up with a college in upstate New York to do a project, and they accepted him. When this happened, I learned I was going to move to America. I wasn't really excited, and I was nervous. I didn't know what was going on because I didn't know what I was going to get myself into. I got my luggage and I went to the airport. When I landed, I realized that I was going to be in a whole different environment.

The moment I realized it all changed was the first day of school. I was always worried about the first day. I was really anxious, and I couldn't talk to anyone because I was too shy. I will never forget the first moment I walked into my social studies class with my dad. I was really nervous, but my teacher acted like he knew me for many years. He said, "Hi" to my dad and smiled. He helped me get rid of my stress by being very kind and welcoming. Still to this day, I'm very thankful for that teacher.

As months passed, my ESL teacher helped me to do better and that's how I got used to the school. She was an angel. She always helped me with everything. I went through hardships with her. My first year went pretty quick since I wasn't really talking to anyone. I learned how to speak English better—my language went from zero to a hundred. I've got Turkish friends too, so I was happy with that.

But in my second year here, that was the time when a coup attempt happened in Turkey. That made it a challenging time for us. My dad got charged with being involved in the coup when we were living in America. They stormed into my dad's university office in Turkey and they threw away his stuff. My dad was really sad because some of his friends were taken into custody. Our whole family was really sad. A lot of people we knew were sent to prison. They were sometimes raped and tortured. So, if we went back to Turkey, we would hundred percent be in prison too, and our lives would be really bad. We were really emotional. Our temporary move turned into a longer one.

After that, my dad was really struggling financially because he was no longer working at the university. His partnership between his university in Turkey and the college got cut, and his salary got affected. We moved to another house in a different part of town to pay less rent. After that, we then gradually started to get some money because my mom and dad sold stuff on online platforms. I had to change schools again. Changing schools again was difficult. I already felt foreign in my current school and now I had to leave the school that I had just got used to for another school. I was confused, and it felt really traumatic at that time.

At the new school, I got international friends, and I had more Turkish friends. Even though it was new, I was still happy in school. But the news coming from Turkey just kept getting worse and worse, so emotionally I was still messed up. We applied for political asylum in America to stay here longer, but then a new law passed saying that if you applied first you will have to go at the end of the line and wait longer. So, we were unlucky again. My family was struggling financially, but as a family we were still trying to be together. We did activities together trying to motivate ourselves.

I think the main thing is that you give up some of your culture and your language at a certain point in the American school. Because you can't understand, in order to understand, you have to take on their lenses and perspective to adapt. You always think about everything in your own cultural way, so you have to learn the other culture to understand other people. My mom, dad, and brother, they all had to get used to it...it is really hard to do that because it's always different at some point. While we were struggling, we weren't completely out of culture since we had our Turkish centers. We would always go there for programs.

At first, when I came here, I had zero English, but now I have better English. Right now, I am writing articles for a magazine. It's a magazine that my friend group started about being Muslim in America. It's a magazine that gives a good source of information for Muslim children growing up in America so they do not forget their culture and religious identity. This magazine is also for every other child to see our values and have fun reading it.

My brother is in college right now. I am hoping that I can also go to college. My parents, they always do everything for us, so I am really thankful for them. I have a beautiful school to go to and a great friend group. It's all good right now. As I grow up here, I hope I can get a job and be independent. I would like to be financially able to afford things so that I can take care of my family better. Since my parents work so hard for me, I would like to pay them back by being independent and strong. I always wanted to be a peace builder. I want to communicate this to my new community and represent kindness and everything that is good.

greencardvoices.org/speakers/Ayse

ASIA
Aden,
Yemen

Manea Almadrahi

Born: Adan, Yemen
Current City: Buffalo, NY

"I THOUGHT EVERYTHING WOULD BE DIFFICULT. THEN, I MET MY TEACHER FOR THE FIRST DAY, AND I SAW A LOT OF STUDENTS, AND THEY WERE JUST LIKE ME. THEY HAVE BEEN THROUGH DIFFICULT SITUATIONS, LIKE ME."

When I grew up in Yemen, I went to school and everything was cool. I remember my life in Yemen before I was ten years old, which was the best part of my life. I remember my childhood and my friends. I remember my neighborhood, and everything about my village, the nearby city. Back in the days when we would travel in Yemen, everything was cool. The roads between the cities from one city to the other city were safe. You could drive safely. You didn't think about anything, but right now the road is full of dangers. Checkpoints, military, and attackers—they are everywhere.

Before, we lived in peace and love. There was no war. We had nothing to be scared about, nothing to worry about—just live our life. We lived our best life. The war started in 2015, and my country is still going through a difficult situation. My mom and my dad decided to think about moving to America. Earlier in life, my dad lived in America for more than 20 years, but we never thought to go to live in America before because we were cool in Yemen. Everything was great there. But after the war began, my dad thought that we needed to move to the U.S. and live with him. My dad went there first. The war was raging when my dad decided to move to the U.S.

My dad, he is just a hard worker. He already had a U.S. citizenship, so his children were eligible to be U.S. citizens too. We had to just pick up our passports from the embassy. Only my mom had to get a visa, but me and my brother were able to get a U.S. passport without a problem. It was very difficult for my mom to get a visa, because she couldn't apply to take her visa because of the law called the "Muslim Ban."

First, when we got our appointment to go to the embassy, they said the only thing we needed was the application for the passport. We went to the embassy on the day of the appointment and they said because of a new law from three months before, called the "Muslim Ban," things would be different. We knew from the news that the "Muslim Ban" was going to happen. Trump and the judge were talking about the "Muslim Ban," so we had to wait for three months, and my mom couldn't get the visa in that time.

I don't remember exactly when we moved, but I think we started our journey in 2017. So, by the time we tried to get the passports again, the war had escalated in our city. We were supposed to travel from our city of Aden in North Yemen to the capital city of Sana'a, where the United States Embassy was. That was the only way they could accept our application for the passport, but because of the fighting, they closed the U.S. embassy in Yemen. So we had to move to another country, Djibouti, in Africa, to finish with all the paperwork. That is where all Yemeni people who need to go to U.S. Embassy have to go and get their passports or visas to get to the United States.

When we traveled, we went from Aden to Djibouti by boat, which was usually used for animals. It was not even meant for people to travel on. When we traveled, I was so scared…everyone was so scared. I know that everyone was scared because it was the first time that we traveled across the sea. My dad was so afraid about that trip. He was in the United States. He said to us, "There is no other way; only by ship." He said it's the only way we can go to Djibouti.

Life in Djibouti was so difficult. The rent was like more than $1,000 for an apartment, and it was only rent. Besides that, there were electricity and water bills. Everything was expensive there. It was so hot and so far from the city. The area was very bad. The electricity was so expensive that from 9:00 in the morning, we were all sitting in the same room so we could save on air conditioning costs. One day a thief came through the window. I swear to God, we were sleeping, and I heard something. He opened the window and came into the room. He saw all of us in the room, and he ran away. I remember that. A lot of people were so bored. When Yemeni people come to Djibouti, they have a lot of money with them, but they also try to save their money. The houses were not that expensive until the Yemeni people came. Then the price went up. When Yemeni people were living in a house, then they knew they had money, so they broke into the houses.

In Djibouti it was so difficult to get an appointment at the U.S. Embassy. We tried to go to get an appointment. Some people got an appointment fast; some people, they have to wait a long time. Some people have been in Djibouti waiting for years—some people for three years, some people since 2015…now it's 2020. We tried to go to and get an appointment to the Embassy. A lot of people spent one year in Djibouti because of the Muslim Ban.

After some time, we got our first appointment with the U.S. Embassy. We get to the embassy, and they say, "Yes, we can give you the passport, but only if your dad can be here." They said we need one parent to sign for the passport, and your mom can't do that because she does not have citizenship and does not have a visa. So my dad had to come from the United States to Djibouti to sign for the passport. At that time, we tried to talk to them about my mom's visa, and they said they can't right now because the Muslim Ban and that we have to wait until the Muslim Ban is over. I don't know…it's strange. During the Muslim Ban, some people get the visa…and some people don't. I don't know why some people get a visa waiver and others don't.

We picked up our passports from the Embassy and waited another month to see if we could get a chance for my mom to get a visa. But the life there was so expensive. The rent was so expensive. The food…everything there was expensive. And the weather was so hot in Djibouti. My dad, he had to get back to U.S. because he ran out of his medicine, and he can't find his medicine in Djibouti, so he had to come back to the United States. My mom told him, "Just go with the kids, and I will stay here. I will wait for my visa." When my mom saw my dad without medicine, she said, "You have to go with the kids, and I will stay here. It's no problem." My dad, he was so afraid to leave my mom and me by ourselves in Djibouti. She said, "Don't worry about it, just go with the kids. I will be fine in Djibouti." It was so hard to leave my mom by herself in Djibouti. Life was so difficult, but we left my mom and moved to the United States. It was such a difficult moment.

We took the airplane from Djibouti to Turkey, Turkey to New York City, and then to Buffalo. When we traveled from Djibouti to the United States, everyone was excited. My brother and my sister, we all sat there smiling, and, at the same time, we were crying. We were excited, but also we missed our mom. Some were also crying with happiness. We got our passports, and we were ready to travel. At the same time, we were crying about my mom because we left her behind…left her in Djibouti.

In Turkey, we waited in the airport for ten hours and then took the next airplane to New York City, then to Buffalo. When I got to Buffalo, my dad had all his family there—everyone came to the airport. Everyone, my family, all my dad's family was there—my uncles, my grandma, and my grandpa. They were all waiting for us. When we got to Buffalo, I was looking out the window of the plane, and I saw Buffalo just covered in snow…all of Buffalo. And, I was so hungry when we got to Buffalo.

From the first day, I was so hungry because I didn't like the food on the airplane. Everyone—my brother, my sister—they all say they don't like the food—and we were so hungry. Then we asked our dad what the famous food in Buffalo is. What do people eat in Buffalo? So, he says there's pizza and chicken wings—that is the famous food in Buffalo. So I told him, "Do you want to buy pizza?" And he said, "For sure!" We went to the pizza shop, and we bought two large pizzas. The next day we slept all day because we were tired from traveling. The next week my dad took us and to get social security cards ready. We stayed at home for a few months, then they were able to register us for the school, and we started going to school.

When I went to school in Buffalo, I was so afraid because I was asking myself, "How am I going to deal with the people? How am I going to deal with the teachers? What am going to say? I don't speak English." It was a difficult moment, and I thought everything would be difficult. Then, I met my teacher for the first day, and I saw a lot of students, and they were just like me. They have been through difficult situations, like me. I met my friends in the school on the first day, and it was not like what I thought because I thought it would be so difficult, but it was cool. The teachers were really friendly. It was very different from the teachers back home.

After that, my mom and all the people, they just went back to Yemen because there's no hope to make it to America. She spent three months in Djibouti and was residing with another family there, but when they went back to Yemen, she went back too. Then, a year later, we heard there are a lot of Yemeni families getting their visas in Djibouti. My mom called us and said, "There are a lot of people who went back to Djibouti, and they got their visa, so why don't we try again?" We asked my mom, " How you are going to make it to Djibouti? Are you going to go by yourself?" She said, "For sure. I will stay by myself. I can go back by myself." So my mom moved back to Djibouti, and then two months later, she got her visa. We were so happy. We were praying for her to make it to the United States, and she was so excited. When she got her visa, we got her a ticket. Then she came, I went to New York City to meet her there. It was the best day!

My life here is good right now. I go to school in the morning, stay in school, and then after school I go to my job. I already got a job here, and all I do is study and work. My life changed a lot when my mom got here. I think there's no way I can live without my mom again. I am not going to leave her; I will stay with my mom forever. My mom is very cool. When she wakes me up in the morning, I go to school. She makes my breakfast—everything is ready, and I just can't think I will ever leave her again. No way.

For the future, first of all, I just want to get my education finished. Without education, you can't know what's right and what's wrong. Once I have education, I will start with my future. Life is better here right now than in Yemen. Some people in Yemen are just finishing their education, and there's no opportunity to get a job or anything. Nothing to do in Yemen when you get your education. When you move to the United States, you have more chances to get a job and to make money. The schools are better here, better than Yemen.

greencardvoices.org/speakers/Manea-Almadrahi

HIGH GRADE
22
BLUE WAY
AFRICA
Jamaame, Somalia

Abdishakur Luhizo

Born: Jamaame, Somalia **Raised:** Camp Kakuma, Kenya
Current City: Buffalo, NY

"ONE DAY I WILL STAND OUT, GO TO MY COUNTRY AND HELP THE KIDS WHO ARE GROWING OR WHO HAVE A PROBLEM. THAT'S MY DREAM. I WANT TO BE A DOCTOR."

I was born in the southern part of Somalia in a small village called Jamaame. We lived there for four years. Then my father decided to move us. It was tough. When I was born, we didn't have a lot of money, but it was good life we were living. My parents, they put all the children together, and they take good care of us. They fight for me. When I was a kid, I was born with a diagnosis called polio. It was tough for my parents to get food, even medicine. They decided to move on to other countries, so they can get help. When they heard about UNHCR, they decided it's a good opportunity to go over there so that I can be healthy and not die.

We moved to Kakuma Refugee Camp and for me, it was a good opportunity to live with the people that are different. We could live like brothers; many families with a lot of people lived over there—people from different countries speaking different languages. We got different religions, but the thing is that we live together, and we survive together—that is something I learned from there. Another thing I learned is to not fight or not make trouble, but to love each other and care about how we live and how we feel. This is good when you live as a refugee, and you say you're different, and you live with a father and mother. We are a family and that gives you a lot of things in life. We care for each other every day and know we are part of a family, even if we die or if we survive. This is how Kakuma people live.

When I was in Kakuma, it was tough because the thing I was so scared of was the teachers because I didn't know how to read and to speak the language of the teacher. Most of us were learning English. At the time, I was a kid and I was speaking Swahili. When you are in school, you need uniforms, pants, or shoes, and if you don't have those things you might get punished a little bit. The school they teach good. Kids are speaking English, and some are speaking their home language, so the teacher is needing to understand what they are saying. For me, I did not understanding of the language, but I wanted to learn. It took time to understand how the education here works and what it means for my life.

When we get out of school, we always play soccer. Sometimes you can see a kid holding a ball in their hand, and you know they're going to play soccer. That is the thing most young kids like to play, so we hope this is going to be our future. It doesn't matter if we don't have anything, soccer can make people happy and make people come together like a union. Even sometimes when we don't have school, we just only play soccer and other games like running or cross country. Those kinds of things we have over there, but our people, they like playing soccer most.

When I was informed we were going to the U.S., my grandma said, "Are you really going to U.S.? You're going to miss me." I was like, "Yeah, I know, but we need something to change in our life. It's a good opportunity when you are going to a different country." I remember many things. My grandma was crying saying, "You are going to U.S." But my other family said, "It's good—you're going change your life. It doesn't matter—you are still our family, and you can call us when you get a phone." I was happy when I heard that we were going to the U.S., I was happy.

On the day of our departure the taxi took us there. We arrived in Kenya, in a place called Nairobi. It was good. It was my first time seeing towers and different cars because the cars were not like the cars in the refugee camp. I was so excited. I thought that if the things I see here are like this when I go to America, it is going to be a whole new future. I was so excited when I got there. Going to America—that was the best feeling…I was really going to the U.S. I was looking at the U.S. people on the TV, and I said, "Wow, it is going to be my whole life like watching them act like in the movie!"

After Nairobi, we arrived in Cleveland. It was my first time on an airplane. I'd never seen an airplane. They treat people good. They give you food that I never knew. This is the life—flying and nobody is touching the ground—you are in the sky! That was good—I liked the plane.

When we arrived in Cleveland, we met our caseworker. Then, she introduced us to our uncles and then my uncle said, "Okay, we make life like a family again here. Do not think family can forget other family—we still are family everywhere we go. You can go every place, but you are still a family. Family can find you." That's what I liked the most in Cleveland when I arrived in America. I saw a lot of different food here, like chicken. I could never eat chicken for a whole day before. I see a lot of different things like clothing. Everything was good. I would say, "Oh, this life is good, you live like a rich person. You have more food, and you got a lot of things. Over there in the refugee camp, you can eat sometimes two or sometimes one time a day. It depends if you have your own money or if the UN gives you a lot of their food. The UN mostly gave us corn and beans. Also flours, salt, oil—those you cook with. Sometimes they give you Kenyan shillings—cash money—like seven or eight hundred (equivalent to $6.36 or $7.26). It depends on your family.

My grandma has a little farm in the camp. She plants a couple of cabbages. Sometimes when we are really tired she says, "Help me to plant these plants." So, we have help her to plow the plant. She tells us it is a good thing when you are farming—your body stays normal and you're not going to be lazy. You always stay in good shape when you farm. When you're farming or playing any sports, it's the same thing.

In Cleveland, I go school, but the school was a little more Spanish than African. The school kinda gives me a hard time—it is hard to understand. I have a lot of friends, and when you have a lot of friends, you make a lot of trouble. My mom says, "Oh you are doing a lot of trouble right now, so you must move on to a different city so I can see you can to do better." Most of the time, I was late getting to the classroom at school. When I came, I do a great job. The problem was that the teacher complained about me being late to school and that is trouble. My mom tells me I must move on. It was seven months when I started being bad. She said before that I didn't grow up with this behavior, so why am I making a switch now? That's why I came to Buffalo. Since I came to Buffalo, I was good. School is good and the teachers always told me, "Don't be late." This time I changed myself. I don't want to be late. I don't want to get in any trouble. I focus on school.

When I'm done with school, I go home, relax, sleep, and do the things that I like in life. You sleep, you relax, you don't need to have trouble. I study in the mornings at school. When I finish, I ask my friends if they want to have fun—that is what I love most in Buffalo. I have friends here. My friends were living in the same community as me in Kakuma. That's when I said, "Oh my God, I am with my family again. I mean, everywhere you go you have family."

My favorite subjects are all the subjects. The thing is, you must focus. It doesn't matter how easy or how difficult—I can do it. Everything is easy to do if you understand, and if you focus, then I think you can do it. That's why I like all the subjects. I feel like they are the same. Sometimes you must fight hard so that you can understand what the different subjects are about.

When I was in Cleveland, I was doing sports, but since I arrived in Buffalo, I must change a little bit my body. I was doing a little bit of gym, then I stopped because I got a little injury. My favorite sport was playing soccer, then I stopped playing soccer.

I started to focus on playing football, after I got information from the school that they need a player to play football. I went to play. They ask me my age and I said, "I'm nineteen." They told me I cannot play, the only people to play are like seventeen years old…like sixteen. I said, "Okay." Even though I'm not doing sports, I can still get my body in shape, like going to the gym, doing push-ups. When I go to college, then I can play my dream.

My goal is to help kids that are diagnosed with different diseases. That's the way I survived—by getting help. I want to help the kids who are growing right now or who are born and need to know how to treat their disease. I want to do this because we know most of the people in Africa do not have a lot of doctors. Kids are dying in different countries. Some of them are mostly in countries like East Africa—Congo, Rwanda, and Kenya. Kids are dying because they are not healthy. The thing is that they give only a little good food for kids. And then medicine in Africa, there's not an easy way to get it. Every time I look at myself, I say, "One day I will stand out and go to my country so I can help the kids who are growing or who have a problem." That's my dream. I want to be a doctor.

greencardvoices.org/speakers/Abdishakur-Luhizo

Science Project
ASIA
Aden,
Yemen

Mysstorah Shaibi

Born: Aden, Yemen
Current City: Rochester, NY

> "THERE WAS SHOOTING NEAR THE WINDOWS, AND WE HEARD SOME SCREAMING AND CRYING NEXT DOOR. THEN A GUY KNOCKED ON OUR DOOR AND HE SAID, 'GET DOWN!' WE DID, AND MY MOM HELD MY SISTER AND MY BROTHER, AND I HELD MY MOM."

My life in Yemen was difficult because my dad lived in America, and I lived with my mom and younger sister and little brother in Yemen. When I lived with my mom, there was not enough money. I did go to school, but I didn't understand anything because I was afraid. I would always sit in the back, and I wouldn't listen. When I come back home, I didn't know what the homework was or what I had to study. My mom didn't know how to read English or Arabic or anything. She couldn't go to school to get educated because there was only her and her mom, and they were poor. She speaks Arabic, but she can't write or read, so no one could help me or teach me. I didn't really care about school when I lived in Yemen.

There was a war in Yemen, and my mom was really scared, and I was scared too. We heard guns and shooting. We lived in a small house with a room and a kitchen. There was shooting near the windows, and we heard some screaming and crying next door. Then a guy knocked on our door and he said, "Get down!" We did, and my mom held my sister and my brother, and I held my mom.

I was the oldest. I took care of my siblings. Every time, I would be the one to go to shop for the house, like food and fries. My dad would send us some money every month. Every year my father would come to Yemen. He would stay like one month with us and then he go back to America. My dad took my older brothers Adbul and Mohammed with him to America because he has a store there. My uncle stayed in America to help with the store when my dad came to Yemen. When my uncle came to Yemen, then my dad would go to America. They would take turns because my uncle have family too in Yemen, so they switched.

My dad and my brothers stayed in America for like one year and then my dad came to Yemen with my brothers. Then one time, he said that we would all go together to America. Then, I was really happy and smiled because we were not going to say goodbye again to each other. We all traveled from Yemen to Djibouti in a boat. We stayed in Djibouti for three months waiting for a visa. Then we traveled to Turkey and stayed there for one day, and then we traveled to America.

In Djibouti, I didn't go to school. We stayed at a hotel—all together in one room. There was not enough space for all of us. It was bad in Djibouti because we didn't know how to eat their food, but there was rice. We couldn't cook in the hotel, so my dad had to bring us food every time. It was bad. We stayed in Djibouti three months and after we got our papers, then we traveled to Turkey.

When I arrived in Rochester my uncle was waiting for us, and he took us to our house. I was surprised because there was a big TV and a couch. I have my own bedroom that I share it with my sister, and I have my own bed. That's the first time I have my own bed. I was really surprised about many things. It was really cold.

My dad worked in the store, and I went to school. The first day I was really nervous and quiet. I didn't know what they were talking about because I didn't know how to speak English. I didn't like it because there were a lot of students who were bothering me. Some students were taking off my hijab. I didn't like it. I told my dad, and my dad said, "Move her to the same class with her brother." I was in sixth grade and my brother, Abdul, was in fifth grade, so I was moved to fifth grade.

My brother Abdul went to America first, and he knows how to speak English a little bit. Once I moved with him to same fifth grade classroom it was better. I have friends over there now. We stayed at that school for two-and-a-half years and then we moved to another school in Brighton. When we moved, I was nervous, but a lot of teachers helped me and then I liked this school. It was really cool. I have friends now. My teacher helped me a lot to learn to speak better English. I read books now! I didn't know how to read in Arabic or English before I came to this school. In Djibouti my dad taught me how to write my name in English, but I always forgot. I know so much more now.

After a year in America, my mom got pregnant and I was really happy because I can see my new sibling. I can see him, and I can take care of him, and I like him. When she was pregnant, she was tired. She didn't wake up with us in the morning or wake up my other siblings to go to school, so I helped with that. I got up at 6:00 a.m. and they got up at 7:00 in the morning. I wake them up and take care of them. I make breakfast and get them ready.

My favorite subject in school is social studies. I like it because sometimes they talk about the war in Yemen and then I can tell them what happened in Yemen. I tell them that it's bad, and I don't like the war because it's really bad. Then they say, "Why?" I say because you're going to hear fire and shootings. I think that surprised the kids in my class because when were they young, they got used to play with toys, but I didn't I have toys, and there was a war.

In our free time, we hang out with my extended family—my aunt and uncle and cousins too. We go to the beach a lot when it's summer, but when it's school, my dad has to go to work, and we have to go to school. In school, my dad tells us to work hard, and he will be proud of me. I said I want to be a doctor, but I don't know because I don't like science. I want to be a nurse because I like to take care of babies.

If I want to be a doctor I need to get better at school and better at science too. I like to be in hospitals because I like to wear gloves and a mask like a doctor. One time my brother had a little bit of a scar here on his finger. I watched the nurse and saw how they took care of the scar. Then when we went home, she gave us extra bandage, and at home I did that for my brother. I was really happy.

greencardvoices.org/speakers/Mysstorah-Shaibi

NORTH AMERICA
Villalba,
Puerto Rico

Sebastian Antonio Berdecia Negron

Born: Villalba, Puerto Rico
Current City: Rochester, NY

"LIFE IN PUERTO RICO WAS SO HARD BECAUSE YOU NEEDED THE ICE TO KEEP THE FOOD COOL SO THAT IT DIDN'T SPOIL. IT WAS BAD BECAUSE THE FACTORY WITH THE ICE WAS FAR FROM WHERE I LIVED. HERE, YOU DON'T NEED TO BRING ICE."

My name is Sebastian. I'm from Villalba, Puerto Rico. I am thirteen years old. I remember, I was born in Ponce, Puerto Rico. My life is a little bit hard because my father drinks; I lost my sister in an accident; Hurricane Maria was bad; my parents struggled. The hurricane happened in September 2017, and we didn't get the lights in my house back on until February 5, 2018. It was bad because my mom worked in Aibonito—a very hilly and mountainous area. It's so far from Villalba, approximately 40 kilometers. I waited after the hurricane, but then I started going to a school in November and went there until July 2018.

Because we didn't have electricity, my momma made me bring the ice from a big factory where they made ice. I went with my mother and my uncle, to bring ice, not just for us but also to my neighbors, to my extended family there. Some people did not have ice money to buy ice, but me and my mom have the idea to help these people.

I remember when I saw what happened after the hurricane, all I saw was the destruction in my town. That was a heartbreak because it's so hard to see your place to be so destroyed by a hurricane. It's so hard. I thought it would be like that the whole time. Later, after the hurricane, I felt bad because I didn't know how much time it will take to repair the destruction. I felt bad, but FEMA came to help. They were nice people. In one school, it's not far from my town, they bring the doctor there. They also gave food to the old people who needed it, but there is only one organization that came and helped.

On January 10, 2018, I have the idea with my mom to come to New York to see how it is in this country and to seek a new life, a new school, and a new home, but in a way, it felt like we went on a vacation. I liked it. We travelled from Ponce to John F. Kennedy Airport in New York City and from John

F. Kennedy to Rochester, New York. I was excited because I had never gone to other country and experience life there. We have a lot of friends and family in Rochester; I have two cousins, and two uncles here.

I finally came to New York again on July 4 in 2019, last summer. I feel good…I feel excited because it's a new country. I am here, but it still feels like I am on a long vacation. I like this place. I feel, "My God, I'm in New York, I can't believe it!" Why I am excited? Because I get to make new friends, meet new people and new teachers and have a new life. Rochester is a beautiful place. My mom is here; she is with me every moment of my life. I love my life here. Rochester is a good place.

Life in Puerto Rico was so hard because you needed the ice to keep the food cool so that it didn't spoil. It was bad because the factory with the ice was far from where I lived. I would have to go there to buy ice in the factory. Here, you don't need to bring ice for the food or the water. When I came here, I was excited to be with my uncle. There was a long time that I did not see my uncle and my cousins. To see them here is good and to stay with them is good for me because in Puerto Rico I was alone in my house. I am with my mom and we are doing well. It was a good to come here. It especially feels good in the summer. I have been here five months now. We have been visiting different places: I went to Syracuse, to Niagara Falls, to the mall, to the market, and, of course, to the school.

Going to school in Rochester feels strange because I was never in a school like this. In Puerto Rico the school is not like this—it's so different. I saw there were not a lot of students here like in Puerto Rico. Here, students are good friends. I go to a bilingual school. There are materials and computers here for the people that speak Spanish or English language. Other things that are different are technology, computers, teachers, materials, and students. The lunch is a lot like in Puerto Rico, but there is more variety here. The teachers are more strict too because they want you to do more, to push yourself, and to have a good future for yourself. It's not like that in Puerto Rico.

I do talk with my friends while I am in my house. I use my phone. I also watch TV and movies. During the lunch at school, I talk with my best friends. It's good too because I do not have brothers. In my house I talk with my cousins and that is good for me. I like to go and spend time with my family, especially when we celebrate something. The days pass quickly when I am with my cousins and my uncles. Life is good—it's nice. We go swim in a big pool, and I love it.

I want to finish this school with nice, good grades. I want to have a great future. I want a job and to help people in Puerto Rico. In the future I want to have a house, a family. That is everything.

greencardvoices.org/speakers/Sebastian-Antonio-Berdecia-Negron

ASIA
Instanbul,
Turkey

Esma Okutan

Born: Instanbul, Turkey
Current City: Rochester, NY

"I CAN STILL REMEMBER WALKING DOWN THE BEACH WITH MY FAMILY, TALKING, DRINKING TEA, AND HEARING THE SOUNDS OF THE SHIPS IN THE BOSPHORUS. IT WAS TRULY BEAUTIFUL."

I was born and raised in Istanbul, Turkey. It is a really beautiful city with amazing historical sites as well as natural beauties. It's partially surrounded by the Sea of Marmara and the Black Sea. I can still remember walking down the beach with my family, talking, drinking tea, and hearing the sounds of the ships in the Bosphorus. It was truly beautiful. Another thing I loved about my country was that it was like a melting pot of European and Asian cultures. One of my favorite activities to do in Istanbul was feeding the stray animals. There were a lot of stray cats and dogs outside and I really enjoyed taking care of them. I lived on the Asian side and I also went to school there. I had most of my family living there too. I was going into the seventh grade before we moved here.

In the summer after sixth grade my family and I were staying in Southern Turkey by the Mediterranean Sea for a vacation with my grandma. I remember that it was a sunny day. I was outside with my brother and when he got back my dad came in and said, "We are moving to the U.S. in two weeks." I was so shocked, and I was like, "What? We're moving to the U.S. in two weeks? It's so soon." He said, "I got a job at Rochester Institute of Technology, so we all will be moving to Rochester, which is a city near Buffalo." I knew my dad had applied for a job in the U.S. but I didn't know any of those names. Realizing our confusion, my dad explained that we will be moving to New York. Then I was like, "Oh, New York, I know New York." I envisioned New York City with big skyscrapers, a lot of people and cars, and I was kind of excited but also a bit nervous.

Even when we went to the airport, I was still nervous. I wasn't feeling overwhelmed that much, but I remember the second we took off I felt really, really sad. I felt like, "Oh this is not just a dream, we are actually leaving and going to New York." We landed at JFK airport in New York City. It was just like I imagined. It was a big, crowded city, and I remember being amazed by the diversity of people and the culture that is so unique to New York City. Me and my family stayed there for one day. The next day we got in a car and drove to Rochester, New York. I remember feeling really confused because the second I got here I was thinking that this is not a big city—it's just a town. For my whole life, I lived in a really big city—Istanbul has fifteen million people. I was shocked that I could see the stars in the sky without having to look up because where I lived in Istanbul, there were always skyscrapers, and I had to look up to see the stars. Here, the houses were so small and all I could see was just trees and sky. It was so beautiful. I felt really happy to come here.

When I left Istanbul, I missed my grandma and my extended family. I actually had a little pet parakeet—a bird named Cicikus. I left him there and that was sad. I basically just left my culture there and my language. I don't use it much. I really liked to write in Turkish, read in Turkish, but when I came here, I couldn't do that as much and that was sad. I had to give up my friends too. Sometimes I would text with my family and my friends, and I would feel really sad that I wouldn't be able to see them for a long time. We thought we would go back in maybe one year or so but my dad got his job for longer, so we just planned on staying longer.

At first, I was really shy, and I didn't want people to hear my English because it was really bad. I didn't join any school clubs or do many activities outside of school, but I had made Turkish friends, so we would go out on the weekend and hang out. After some time, I got more adjusted to the culture and the language, and I started to go to many school clubs. Now I am a writer for the school newspaper paper club. I joined many other clubs such as Math Team, International Club, and Art Club. I join the Math Team more regularly.

I haven't decided about what I want to be when I grow up. Right now, I'm really into chemistry and history, so I might do something related to those subjects. I want to go to a good college and get a good job and be independent. Other than that, I'm really interested in children's rights, especially for refugee children. I feel like all that I have gone through opened my eyes to the struggles refugees and immigrants face coming here. I would be so happy to show them that they are not alone and to help them in any way that I can.

greencardvoices.org/speakers/Esma-Okutan

AFRICA

Muyinga
Gasorwe Refugee
Camp, Burundi

AFRICA

Ndunda,
Democratic
Republic
of the Congo

Mireille & Mery Nabukomborwa (Sisters)

Born: Camp Muyiga Gasogwe, Burundi (Mireille);
Ndunda, Democratic Republic of the Congo (Mery)

Current City: Buffalo, NY

MERY: "IT WAS DIFFICULT BECAUSE PEOPLE IN THE CAMP DID NOT HAVE ENOUGH FOOD TO EAT...I LIVED IN ONE HOUSE OF THIRTEEN PEOPLE AND THAT FOOD WAS NOT ENOUGH TO FEED ALL THE PEOPLE.

MIREILLE: "TO GET WATER, IT WAS DIFFICULT...TO FIND WATER YOU HAVE TO CLIMB THE MOUNTAIN TO GET WATER. IT WAS FAR AWAY."

Mery: I was born in a village in Congo called Ndunda on August 5, 2002. My parents told me we moved from Congo because there were people killing other people and because we don't have freedom. We moved to Burundi. We stayed in the camp in Burundi for fifteen years.

Mireille: I was born in Burundi in a camp on September 10, 2004. My parents told me my native country is Congo, but I was born in Burundi. They moved to Burundi because they wanted freedom and wanted a place that we can have an education. In Congo, if you go to school you have to pay money. They didn't have money, so they moved to Burundi because there is free education.

Mery: I have my mom, dad, two brothers, and four sisters. One brother is two years older than me. Mireille is younger than me and another sister is fifteen years old. Another brother is eleven. One sister is seven years old and another is three years old. At the camp I started school when I was seven years old. I would wake up every day in the morning and cleaned myself and go to school. We walked to school. It was difficult because people in camp did not have enough food to eat, but someone bring us food. The UNHCR gave us ten pounds of flour and three pounds of beans each month. In my family, I lived in one house of thirteen people and that food was not enough to feed all the people. Life was difficult for all people in the camp.

Mireille: To get water, it was difficult. In the summer, you had to climb the mountain to get water. It was far away.

I would wake up every morning to go to the choir. When I come from the choir, I have to wash the dishes and go to the school. In high school we went to the school in the afternoon. I would play games with my friends. I know many activities and many games. On the holidays we eat together like a family or a group of friends. Some of the games we played were monkey-in-the-middle, soccer, and one game called kange. When you play kange, it's just like you're doing competition with another group. Your group is on one side and the other group on the other side. You jump and put your legs up.

Mery: Immigration called us to go for an interview with our family. You have to go to interview with the White people to start to go to America. I went to the office with my family and we sat together, then the White people started the interview. They told us we have to go to another village called Muyinga to interview again. Then we waited three months or six months, and then they brought us the paper to go to the interviews in the capital city, Bujumbura When we got interviewed, people in the government of America say, "yes," but we have to wait seven months or one year. So, we wait in the camp. When the immigration letter came, we went to the capital city in Burundi. When we go there, we start interview again. Then the White people told us we have to wait again in the camp. We wait to see if America will say yes or no. If yes, we have to go to America, or America can say no. But America said "yes". We went to the hospital to check if we have diseases in our body, and then the hospital called IOM told us that we don't have any member of the family who has disease. The doctor told us we have to go to the Camp to wait. Then my brother Bwemere told us we have to go back to the capital city to check if me and my brother have disease. We go back two weeks and we go back in the camp again.

Mireille: I was thinking to come to America because I saw a picture from friend that they have a good life when they moved to America. I was thinking it can be good to go to America because you can make a better life. When we found out we can come to America, my sister and my older brother were in the hospital in the capital city because they thought we have to go to the hospital to check if they have disease in their body. When they were in the hospital, they called my mom. She had to come to the hospital because they were too young and they cannot stay by themselves there. So, we stayed with my three cousins, and my three sisters and one brother in the house with my father while my mother went to the hospital.

On April 26, 2008 one man come to our house. He told us that we have to go to the capital city and take the airplane to go to America. That was the twelfth day since my sister and my brother were in the capital city, so we called my mom to tell her she had to come back to prepare everything so we could move. My mom gave everything we had in the house, like clothes, to a friend. We got in the car and we went to the capital city, Bujumbura. We stayed one week in the hospital to take medicine and then took the airplane from Bujumbura. We went to Addis Ababa in Ethiopia and then took another plane to Washington, D.C. Then we took another plane to Buffalo. In the airplane, they speak English, and it was difficult for us to talk to people to get water or food, or to go to the restroom. It was difficult for us to travel to America.

Mireille: The first day when I got to the United States, I was very hungry because I didn't eat the airplane food for two days. The food was new for me. I didn't know what food I could eat, and I was sick. When we got to the airport in Buffalo, I saw my uncle for the first time in my life because he had lived ten years in America. I saw my uncle and caseworker waiting for us; they took us to their car. We got into their car and they showed the house and how to use the stove.

When I was in the camp, I thought we had to live in buildings in America because people who lived in the camp and moved to America sent us the picture they took in downtown. They also told us they live in a tall building, so I thought I have to live in a tall building too. But when I got here, they gave us a house, and it was a surprise for me. In the camp we didn't see the beds in America. The bed is uncomfortable in the camp. The bed here is good to sleep in. In the camp, there is a disease called a maupele (pimples). It's just when something grow on your body and it is a disease that can affect you and you have to go to the doctor.

Mery: In the first week when we got in the house, everything was new to us—the stove was new...the bathroom was new. The first week when my uncle came to visit the house, where we stay with my mom and dad, he would take my parents to appointments. When my mom and my dad left to go to the office with him, we stayed—me, my brother, and little sisters. One day some person came to the house who we didn't know. We don't open the door because we don't know him. We went under the bed to hide because my mom and dad told us that we don't open the door when they're not there in the house with us. When the man was gone, we looked out the window and saw his car gone. My sister was sleeping downstairs, so we told her to come back upstairs with us. Our uncle told us in America you don't have to open the door to people. The person had come to fix the bathroom because the bathroom was broken, but we didn't know it was him.

Mireille: We went to the park with my uncle because he knows Buffalo very well. He came to take us to the market. Sometimes we went to his house to play with our cousins. In the first week we went to the church, but we didn't understand what they were singing about. In the camp, I was a leader in the choir in my church. My favorite song in Swahili is called "Yesu Mipakan." The song is about when a man asked Jesus if you can divorce your wife if she is cheating. The man said Moses told them that if you find your wife cheating, you have to give her a divorce. They were asking Jesus if that was true or false. Jesus told them about marriage and divorce. He said Moses was telling the truth and he came to keep Moses' promise.

When we came here to Buffalo, it was May 5, 2018. We went to school in September. Everything was new. We didn't understand anything. When people would talk to us, we'd say, "Hi, hello, how are you doing?" We would say this because in my country, the teacher taught us how to say, "Hi, hello, I'm from… and my name is." But when people come to talk to you, we don't understand anything, so we had to be quiet and listen.

When it was September, the caseworker told us we have to go to Lafayette High School to study. The first day was good because we found other people who talk in Swahili. I was studying in ninth grade. The first day when I came here to my classroom, no one spoke Swahili. There was one girl speaking Kinyarwanda and it was too difficult for me. I tried to speak to her because she was almost one year in Buffalo, and ask her to tell me what they're talking about. It was good because of some teachers here, Ms. Wallace helped me to learn how to speak English and when I don't understand, she told me how to go Google Translate what she's talking about. Now, I'm better at speaking English.

Mery: In ninth grade, my favorite subject was English because I was studying in Ms. Cooper's class, and she helped me learn how to speak English. When I don't understand something, she tells me to go to Google Translate and translate what she is talking about. Ms. Cooper helped me to learn more English.

Mireille: In ninth grade, my favorite subject was English because my teacher was good. She was trying to help everyone understand what they were talking about. Now my favorite subject is Global Studies because I want to learn more about history.

Mery: My future…my dream…is that I want to be a doctor because I want to help people. If people have a disease, I want to help fix it. I want to help us all to live a good life. I want to study hard to be a doctor. In my camp, education was not good, but I came here to get a better education, and I want to help people. We thank God for everything he has done for us. Never give up your dreams.

Mireille: I want to be a doctor because in my country some people need help. Some have diseases, and they never go to the doctor. If I become a doctor, I can help other people. My life would be better because I can get more money to build a house or to make something for my family. Some people in my family are poor; they don't have food to eat, so I have to help them because they helped me in the past. I want to thank God for everything he has done for us. I thank the people who will read my story. If you have something you want to do in the future, don't give up on your dream. You have to fight for your dream.

Mery: I want to thank all the teachers in the Newcomer. They work very hard to make sure every student understands. Even if you don't speak English they have to help you. All the people who are reading this I want to tell you never give up on your dreams. Even if people let you down, you have to get up and start again. Be what you want to be. Don't let people work against your dreams. You have to work hard and let all people know you can do it.

greencardvoices.org/speakers/Mireille-Mery-Nabukomborwa

MEMBERS ONLY
ASIA
Aden,
Yemen

Abdulmageed Shaibi

Born: Aden, Yemen
Current City: Rochester, NY

"WHEN I WENT TO THE SCHOOL THE FIRST TIME, I WAS VERY NERVOUS. I DIDN'T KNOW ANY ENGLISH...I WASN'T UNDERSTANDING ANYTHING. I WAS NERVOUS AND DIDN'T KNOW WHAT TO SAY. EACH OF THEM WAS SPEAKING TO ME, BUT I DIDN'T KNOW WHAT TO SAY."

My life in Yemen was not very good because of the war. The schools are not very good either. The teachers hit you, and there was not enough food. The electricity...it just works for just one hour a day. My dad was in America, and I was with my mom and five siblings in Yemen. My dad was calling my mom and saying, "When I go back to America, we will go together." I was very happy and excited waiting for him to come back. When he came back, he said that we will take two of our neighbors, Sultan and Majboor, with us as well. The reason we came to the U.S. is because of the war and hunger. There wasn't a lot of food in Yemen. I left my grandma on my mom's side in Yemen. I left my home, my friends, and school.

On the day of our big journey, my whole family and our two neighbors went first to Djibouti with a big boat across the sea. Djibouti is another country—it's in East Africa. It was my first time going to Djibouti, and I was kind of dizzy. The second day was a little bit better, but the food wasn't very good on the boat, and there was very little of it. When we got to Djibouti, we stayed one day in the airport and slept on the floor because there were no beds. We waited, then after a while, we went into the hotel. We stayed there for three months.

Djibouti had a beach, and we would go there every day. The beach was clean but weird too—at night the water goes way up, and in the morning, it goes way down...and there's nothing. We went to the airport again to go to America. We went on the airplane, and it was my second time on the airplane. It was better the second time because I had my siblings to talk to—the first time, I wasn't with them; I just was with my brother and dad. My siblings were excited with me. We laughed together. They were very happy they were on the plane. When we went to America, we went to New York City first. After we stayed in New York City, we went to Rochester, New York. We stayed for one week, not going to school or doing anything. Then, after that, we started going to school, and life is good.

The first time I left to go to America was very bad because my dad said, "You will go with just me and your brother." I was kind of not very happy because I would be leaving my mom and my other five siblings there in Yemen. I was kind of sad, but when we got to the airport, I was better because I saw the airplane. It was my first time on an airplane. I was very happy, but when we got in the airplane, I was kind of sick. It was my first time on an airplane because in Yemen, we don't travel a lot because there's not a lot of money. When we landed in New York, my Dad was thinking we would just drive to Rochester, but I told him I was very sick, and I didn't want to go in a car. Then, he said, "We will stay one day in the hotel in New York."

It was kind of cold in New York. In Yemen, it's very hot. When I woke up and looked out the windows, everything was very, very different. The cars have spots to park in, but in Yemen every car parks where there is free space. Everything was organized in America, but in Yemen it's not organized. Then, my dad drove to Rochester with a car, and I wasn't very sick like I would be if he was driving the car in Yemen. I was cold and my brother was cold. Then, my dad said we will go to the mall to buy coats. Then, it was warm with the jackets because they were very good quality jackets. My dad already knew English because he came to America more times than us. When we go to Rochester, there were different people there that I didn't know but they were from Yemen. I ended up living with them for two years and a half.

When I went to the school the first time, I was very nervous. I didn't know any English. When I went into the school, the students were very different. I went inside the class and the students that I was with were talking, but I wasn't understanding anything. I was nervous and didn't know what to say. Each of them was speaking to me, but I didn't know what to say. Then, I needed to go to the bathroom, and I went to the teacher. I didn't know how to ask. I was trying to say it in Arabic, but he didn't understand me. He had his phone with a Google translator, and I told him in Arabic. Then, he understood it. Later the bell rang, but I didn't know why. In Yemen, they have a bell at school that the principal rings to tell you the school starts. My teacher said it was time for lunch. When we went to lunch, the lunch was very different, and I didn't know how to get it, and they had to teach me. It was very good, and I liked the lunch.

My life now is very, very good because of my family, and my teachers are really nice to me. My school is like…the best! My dad said it's the best school, and the school is really very good. I go to school every day. I stay at home for most of the time when I am not in school—I don't go to work. For most of the time, it's just school and home. My favorite subject is math. I liked math when I was in my country too. Over here, it is a little bit harder because it was different. I stay after school sometimes with my teachers to do work or to do other things with them. Then, I go home.

Sometimes, my dad takes me to work with him for like two hours to wash the dishes. My dad owns a store. It has the best chicken wings in Rochester. It's very good. I told my dad I need a new phone and then he said, "If you want a new phone, then you have to work." I said, "Okay, I'll work." It's not very hard work. It's easy. Then, he gives me money.

On Saturday and Sunday, I stay home and play Fortnite. I love these games. I have an iPhone. In Yemen, I didn't have anything. Over here, life is very good. It's my first time playing games on something like a device. I watch YouTube and I listen to music—hip-hop music mainly. In the summer, life is very good because Ms. Halligan, my teacher, gives us free passes to go the swimming pool, and we go there most of the time. I just went to the pool one time in Yemen, but here I went almost every day in the summer. I was very happy that we have passes and that we go there. The pools are very different from Yemen, and they have rules. In Yemen, there is no rules. I was very happy in the pool. My mom came with us because we have to have a guardian with us.

My dream for the future is that I want to be like my dad, own a big store. I don't want to stay in America for the rest of my life. I want to go back and forth to Yemen and to America.

greencardvoices.org/speakers/Abdulmageed-Shaibi

ASIA
Jashore,
Bangladesh

Anika Khanam

Born: Jeshore, Bangladesh
Current City: Buffalo, NY
Raised: Jhenaidah, Khulna Division, Bangladesh

"MY GOAL IS TO CHANGE THE LIVES OF THE HOMELESS AND OTHER GROUPS OF PEOPLE WHO ARE STRUGGLING BY CONVINCING AND EDUCATING THE SOCIETY AT LARGE."

My name is Anika Khanam, and I was born in the south eastern part of Bangladesh in the city of Jashore. My parents were also born in Bangladesh. I have a little sibling, a sister, her name is Roussa. When I was two years old, my parents and I had to move to my grandpa's house because my dad got a job working for a private company, and he had to change places frequently. So, I grew up in Jhenaidah in Khulna division about two hours from my birth city.

When I was five years old, my parents took me to the school for the first time. It was amazing for me to meet new friends, but it was a little bit scary, too. The scary part was the journey to and from school—especially the walk going there and coming back. That was a route I'd never followed before, so it was new to me. But the school itself was fun. I love to talk to people, so I met a lot of people in the school. It was exciting. I had a best friend; her name is Saddiya. I don't like her mom because her mom always tells Saddiya to be more like me because I always did my homework, and she didn't.

I remember that when I was five years old, I moved to my grandpa's house. We had a lot of fun there. I never got alone time when I lived with my parents—only sometimes when my parents would go out. I like to be alone. My parents always supported me and always taught me. They would say, "One day you will have to stand on your own. When you grow up and nobody is with you, you will have to learn how to stand by yourself, be independent. You have to learn to manage everything." My parents teach me all of this.

My mom always helped me to study because I cannot study by myself. Sometimes my mom gets busy with work, and then I get a bad grade. That's when I realized how it feels to lose something. In my life, I never like to lose, so I set a new goal every day. Every day I when wake up, I make a goal that I have to do "this…this…and this." If I achieve it, then I feel so much better. I don't like to lose—no…never. It's important to lose in life, I understand, but I never want to.

There are many reasons why we left. First of all, in Bangladesh so many people live there, and they don't have that much resources. Also, the school wasn't very good. If you want a better education, you have to go to a private school and that will cost you a lot of money. My parents wanted my sister and I to have a better education. So an important part of why we left was because the educational system there was not good. Also, we didn't have that much money and had some financial problems. My parents wanted us to lead a better life. Therefore, we decided to immigrate to the United States. My uncle lived in the U.S., and he was the one who helped us come here.

I was thirteen years old when my mom told me that we were going to the U.S. I was so happy. Everybody told me that I should value this chance. I know how it feels when you don't have opportunity, but you have certain skills. Moving to America was a little bit sad for me. It was hard to leave Bangladesh because I had to leave all the things that I got used to and get settled in a new place. When I first came here, it was amazing, but I was so scared because I didn't understand what people were saying. I was happy, but I missed my friend Saddiya. Now, if my friends text me and say, "I miss you," I say, "Don't miss me because I will meet you soon."

We took three planes. We started in Bangladesh, and after landing in Turkey, we got on another plane and came to New York City. Then, we got on another plane to come to Buffalo. My aunt was waiting for me and my family at the Buffalo Municipal Airport to welcome us. My cousins were so excited because we were coming. I met my cousins only once before when I was a kid, but that time was so long ago that I don't even remember them. I knew their names, and I had talked to them on the phone sometimes, but I never saw them, so I was excited, too!

After we arrived, we stayed home for about two days because my relatives kept on coming to see us and to see what we're doing. Then, on the third day we walked outside and went to a store to buy a few things. I bought ice cream because I love ice cream. One week after we came, it started to snow—and I loved it! I had never seen snow before, but it was so cold, so I didn't go outside, but I enjoyed watching the snowfall through the window.

One month after we arrived, I started to go to American school. The first day that I went to school was a little bit easy for me because I tried to understand, and I understood everything. I was so shy, and I couldn't talk, but I understood everything. I didn't expect to have a good day that day, but it was better than I expected. Then I started to go every day, and I worked really hard. I was placed in an ESL class. When the teacher realized that my English was better than my level, they placed me in the next level, and I didn't take ESL classes anymore. There were a lot of people, but no Bengali people who could help me. It was good for me in a way because I got the opportunity to learn by myself, so I believe that when you don't have any people to rely on, you learn how to be on your own, how to stand up for yourself, and be independent.

I realized that I had to learn. I had to do hard work because I needed to learn everything in order for me and my family to survive. I started to learn the language. At first, I used the google translator, and I watched a lot of videos. Some days I took notes, and when I started to go to the school, I didn't know what to say, but I took those notes. The notes helped me to know to say, "this… this…and this." Because I needed to learn, I took notes and then started to improve.

I've been here for one year now. I like to read books, do my schoolwork, and I also like to draw. I like to draw because it helps me express my feelings and my thoughts. I want to give life to my feelings and ideas—it is my passion! I also like to solve math problems. I have cousins who help me all the time. I am so lucky to have people to help me, but I understand that when people don't have anyone to help them, it is hard. When I grow up, I want to be someone who can help people. I want to work for the kids who live on the street—homeless people and kids—and I want to give them a better life. I know a lot of people who have good, quality skills, but they never get the opportunity—especially in my country, there are a lot of people like that. Now there are even more people living there because of things happening in Myanmar. Many refugees came from Myanmar and are now staying in Bangladesh.

I want to talk about my dreams, and what I have learned so far in my life. When I was five years old, my grandpa and grandma on my mom's side died. My grandpa died of cancer. Before he died, he told me that I had to be a doctor because the medical treatment was really bad and that I needed to be someone who can help others. So when I grow up, I want to be someone who can help others. My parents also want me to be a doctor. I also want to be a social worker who can help people in need. I want to go back to my home country and work with people who need help. In addition, I want to live with people who need help because I want to really understand how it feels to be homeless.

I can understand, but I want to experience it, too.

Also, I know I have a long way to go. I still don't know many things and don't have any clear plan, but I know that the changes I want to make, I cannot make by myself. I have to convince people to join me by talking to them, by showing them. I know I cannot change people's ways, but I can change their feelings. So, I'm working on it. In the future, I want to make an organization—start small and grow it. I know it is a long ways away, but that is my dream and hopefully I will reach my goal one day. My goal is to change the lives of the homeless and other groups of people who are struggling by convincing and educating the society at large.

Having peace in my mind is important to me, so when I get angry, I love to draw pictures. I also write letters in a notebook, then rip them out and throw them away. Afterwards, I start to focus on my work again because I believe that in your life a lot of people will come and try to convince you to change your ways. But you have to be focused, but still try to do new things every day because in your life you can learn a lot of different things. Don't stop learning. Every day you wake up, you start learning. And never listen to people, who try to convince you to do bad things. Love yourself.

greencardvoices.org/speakers/Anika-Khanam

NORTH AMERICA
Bayamón,
Puerto Rico

Yanielys Marie Nieves Rivera

Born: Bayamon, Puerto Rico
Current City: Rochester, NY

> "I WAS IN FLORIDA WHEN HURRICANE MARIA CAME ON SEPTEMBER 20, 2017...MY MOM AND SISTER WERE IN PUERTO RICO. THEY LIVED THROUGH THIS HURRICANE WITHOUT WATER AND ELECTRICITY. I FELT BAD THAT I CAN'T HELP. I COULDN'T MAKE THEM SAFE."

My name is Yanielys Marie Nieves Rivera but everybody calls me Marie. I was born in Puerto Rico. I am from Bayamon in the northern part of the island. My life in Puerto Rico was good. I lived with my mother and my big sister. School was good because I could understand everything. Sometimes school was not good, when the teacher was angry. On the weekends I stay with my friends.

I was living with my mother and my sister in Puerto Rico, and this whole time my father was staying in the United States. He lived here for fifteen years. When I was twelve years old my mother asked me if I wanted to go and live with my father. I said yes because I never had a chance to live with my father, so I came to stay with my father in the United States—in Florida, specifically.

I took an airplane from Puerto Rico to Florida. When I arrived in Florida my father was waiting for me at the airport. When I arrived in Florida it was good because I liked to go to amusement parks in the summer and that was good, but when I started school again in seventh grade, I didn't like it because I didn't understand anything, so it was difficult.

I was in Florida when Hurricane Maria came on September 20, 2017. My family—my mom and sister—were in Puerto Rico. They lived through this hurricane without water and electricity. I worried about them a lot. I felt bad that I can't help. I couldn't make them safe. After Hurricane Maria passed, my mom and my sister moved to Rochester, and I went to Rochester with them. My father is in Florida. He has an apartment in Florida with my stepmother. My sister later went back to Puerto Rico with her boyfriend, so I live with my mom. Now I am in 9th grade. School is the same—I still don't understand the language very well.

My life now is good because I have new friends. I like the school because it is different from Florida. The school in Florida was difficult because it's all in English, but here in Rochester school is different because the school is bilingual—it's in Spanish and English. I enjoy the time with my friends. On the weekends, I stay with my uncle and my cousin. We do shopping or something like that.

When I graduate, I want to go to Puerto Rico and help my country. I want to finish university and study in the field of gynecology or pediatrics. I want to help mothers and babies.

greencardvoices.org/speakers/Yanielys-Marie-Nieves-Rivera

AFRICA
Nyarugusu,
Tanzania

Estel Neema

Born: Kigoma Region, Tanzania
Current City: Buffalo, NY
Raised: Nyarugusu Refugee Camp, Tanzania

"WE WOULD HAVE TO WAKE UP EARLY EVERY MORNING AT 5:00 A.M. BECAUSE WE HAD TO FETCH WATER BECAUSE THERE WAS NO WATER IN THE HOUSE. SOMETIMES, IF THE WATER WAS TOO DIFFICULT TO GET, WE WOULD WAKE UP IN THE MIDDLE OF THE NIGHT, LIKE 2:00 A.M. TO GO FETCH WATER."

My name is Estel Neema, and I was born in Kigoma Region in Tanzania, but both of my parents were born in Democratic Republic of the Congo. They told me they came to Tanzania in 1996 because there was war in Congo and because they had no place to live in the eastern Sud-Kivu region of Congo. And because there was fighting, they told me that some people died and that some survived, they fled and started living in the refugee camp in Tanzania called Nyarugusu. All the kids from my family, including me, were born in the camp. There were a lot of families there. We lived there, and despite this not being our country, we had a new life. My parents tell me that in Congo life was good... they lived...they enjoyed their life. But I don't know what it was like in Congo because I've never been there. I don't know what it's like.

In my camp, there were a lot of people, a lot of different ethnicities—Warundi, Sukuma, Banyamulenge. We spoke a lot of different languages but mostly we have two languages. For many years there were mostly Congolese people there; however, in 2015 many Burundian refugees arrived as well. The camp was so big. It had 150,000 people, many living with their families. It was a lot of us. It was huge. In the camp, I lived with all my family members: mom and dad, my three brothers and five sisters, and my grandma, and my grandpa. Life there was hard. Getting food and other items that you needed was hard. We had to work on a farm to get food for my family to eat. We had no running water and had to go to the river to get water, which was not clean. UNHCR would give us clean water sometimes, but a lot of times the water was dirty. There were a lot of diseases there because the water was dirty. The camp was not clean at all. There was no proper sanitation, garbage disposal...nothing like that. People got a lot of diseases from the dirty water—mostly malaria, but sometimes Ebola, sometimes cholera. Long time ago, we had a lot of help, but when they started sending us to America and the number of Congolese refugees was going down, there was less and less help. When you got sick, getting medicine was especially hard. You could go to the hospital and you could stay in the hospital, but you could not get anything to help you get better. They could not give you medicine because they didn't have it.

We would have to wake up early every morning at 5:00 a.m. because we had to fetch water because there was no water in the house. Sometimes, if the water was too difficult to get, we would wake up in the middle of the night, like 2:00 a.m. to go fetch water. Then, at 6:00 a.m. we would stay up cleaning the entire place where we lived. Then by 7:00 a.m. we washed the dishes from breakfast and then to school. School would last five hours. There was not enough room for everyone, so if you're in first grade to sixth grade, you go in the morning, and all other grades go in the afternoon.

On the day that I was told we were going to America I felt so different, like it was a dream. The camp had an area where they would put up different announcements, including a list with names of people who were approved to go to America. If you saw your name on the list of people going to America, you would be so happy, so very happy. When my father came and told us, he saw our family name on the list and that we're going to America, the whole family was screaming with happiness. We were screaming, "We're going to live in the United States of America!" I don't know how to explain it—I felt so happy and was about to cry. I was so happy to come to America. Our neighbor was crying though because we were going to leave them and they would be lonely without us, but it was very good for us. My grandparents would not be going with us though, we left behind in the camp when we came to the U.S.

Our journey was really long. It takes some people a week to get to the U.S., but our journey took like a month. We first went to Kasulu City in Tanzania, and we stayed there for three days. Then they told us we had to move to Kigoma, so we went shopping and bought all the things that we needed. We stayed in Kigoma for three weeks and were then sent back to Kasulu again. We went back, about a day, before going to Dar es Salaam, which is the capital of Tanzania, where we stayed one week. We brought all our documents with us, but we lost them, so we had to stay in Dar Es Salaam longer, until we got the documents back.

Some people take a plane from Dar es Salaam to the U.S. directly, but we went from Dar es Salaam to South Africa, then came to New York City and finally to Buffalo, New York. The journey was hard, really hard, but we had to do it because we had to come.

In the airplane, I felt…I don't know…that I was used to living the village life. The food was…I don't know, I just didn't like it. It was my first time eating that kind of food, so it didn't even taste good to me. I am not even sure what kind of food it was. It looked like fish, and I don't like fish. And the bathroom…I didn't know how to ask to go to the bathroom. The people on the airplane all spoke different languages, and while we spoke two languages, none of them were the languages spoken by the people on the airplane, so I didn't know how to ask to go to the bathroom in a way they could understand me. So, in the end, we didn't ask about using the bathroom. We just found it on our own.

When we landed in Buffalo, there were people waiting for us, our case workers—two girls, Swahili speakers from Kenya, and one man. They knew how to find us because we had an "IOM bag." Because our family is big, we had to take two cars and half of our group, the ones in a van, got lost.

When we arrived in America, it was like, "Wait…what? This is America?" It was different—I thought it was going to be somewhere like in heaven. They showed us the house…they showed us the food…they showed us how to use the TV and phones and all of that. It did feel like the heaven a lot of people talked about back in the camp. They told us, "In America you can do everything. You can do whatever you want. People will give you free things." So, yes, in some ways, it felt like heaven.

So many things were new to us. The bathroom, we were used to a little because we used that kind of bathroom in Dar es Salaam when we stayed there, but the stove was new to us. When we first came, they cooked for us, and there was a lot of food that was already cooked in the fridge. We didn't start using the stove until a month after we arrived. At first, we were scared we were going to burn the house down. We felt comfortable using it only after the caseworker came and told us how to use it.

The first week, we felt our life was so different because in my camp, we didn't stay in the house all day. Instead, we would wake up and start working! We also wouldn't just stay in the house when it was dark because there is no electricity there. There, you would just be inside and go and sleep. But here, we would just wake up and stay in the house all day. It felt kind of different and weird, but we got used to it. My day in the camp was all about fetching the water and going to school. We came to the U.S. in the summer when it was the summer break, but we didn't start school until the end of September. Our neighbors were Congolese, but we didn't know that until we started going outside. Some of our new neighbors spoke Swahili and some didn't. Our neighbors helped us with a lot of stuff.

At first, we didn't actually go out of the house. After we were in America for like a month, we started taking care of ourselves and went outside more. When we needed something, a caseworker would send someone to help us, but in general we stayed home most of the time. The caseworkers helped us to go to the store and buy stuff because we didn't have a car. They also taught us how to use the bath, how to shop in a store, and how to use the NFTA. They taught us all these things and were so helpful.

The first day of school I was nervous. All the kids, they spoke English, and I was the only one who didn't speak English. I went to International School 45, an elementary school. When they asked me something, I didn't even know what they were saying. Sometimes I got bullied because I didn't speak English. That's what I remember about starting school. But I got used to it, and when I started speaking English, we all became friends.

After some time, winter came. In the beginning it just felt normal. I had never seen snow before, so I said, "What the heck is this?" I didn't know… I'd never thought of my neighborhood looking like this—all white and covered in snow. It was my first time seeing snow. Our neighbors helped us by giving us jackets and jeans and warm stuff like that because we were just wearing skirts like we would in the camp.

My life now that I have been here for three years is so different. I go to school. My favorite subject is actually math. On weekends, I like to go out with my friends, play together with them, or go visit my friends' house. We spend the weekends together. Now, my life is all about going to school every week. My father has a car and a job; my mother used to work but she had to get surgery and after they said that she cannot work anymore so only my father works. My brothers and sisters are all good, they all go to school, so we only get to see each other in the afternoon. The only thing I miss are my friends, that's it. I had a lot of friends in Tanzania, and I miss them. Now in Tanzania, I only talk to my family members, the one we left behind. Talking to my friends is hard because they don't have phones.

In the future, I want to become an actress, that's what I like. I just really like acting. When I see people acting, I want to do that. I like movies, and I feel like I can do any kind of movies. I love American movies, and I watch a lot of African movies, too. I like to watch different movies. American shows that I watch sometimes are *Stranger Things*, *The Hate You Give*, and others. I am learning a lot.

greencardvoices.org/speakers/Estel-Neema

ASIA
Aden,
Yemen

Sultan Yahya

Born: Aden, Yemen
Current City: Rochester, NY

"BRIGHTON HELPED ME BECAUSE ALL OF MY FRIENDS SPEAK DIFFERENT LANGUAGES, AND WE ALL SPEAK ENGLISH TOGETHER, TO ONE ANOTHER. BRIGHTON TEACHERS TAUGHT ME HOW TO READ AND WRITE."

My life in Yemen when I was a kid was so good, but as I was growing up, when I was nine, the war started, and bad things happened. But when I was a kid it was so good because I lived out in the country. I was a farmer and shepherd. I liked to go mountain biking with my friends. We had fun with our bikes in the mountains! We used to do that a lot. The school I really liked it, but the teachers, they did like to hit any student if he didn't do his homework or he came late or if he didn't cut his hair or if his nails were dirty, they would hit him.

I used to live in the country, but occasionally I stayed in the city. I would move back and forth. I didn't stay in one place. After the war broke out, I used to stay in the country more, but because of the war, I didn't get to the countryside as much. When I went to school in the city, they don't hit students, except if they were in big trouble. After the war broke out, I used to stay in the country more because the war didn't get to the countryside as much. I used to take the sheep to the mountains, and sometimes I would bring the cows and the donkey with my mom.

When I was eleven years old, my mom told me that I will go with my neighbors to America. I was so happy because I heard a lot about America. It was so good, and I was most excited about the snow because I have never seen snow. In the countryside we sometimes get ice, if it falls from the sky. So ice comes sometimes but not snow—never snow. My uncle, he is my neighbor, and his son, he is my cousin Adbul—they came from America to visit. I was so happy because he is my best friend. I was so happy. We would just go mountain biking together because he is the same age as me, and he also sometimes went to school in the city and to the countryside. Abdul and my uncle were in Yemen for maybe a year. After that, we all went to America together.

I was thinking about it: I was feeling bad and feeling good. I was feeling bad that I was going to have to leave my mom and my two sisters, all my friends, and my school, but I couldn't learn too much Arabic because of the war. I couldn't go to school every day; in fact, I sometimes would go to school only one day in a week. Sometimes I wouldn't go for a whole week because they had to close the schools because of the war. I was excited to go to America, but I was sad at the same time.

We began our journey by travelling by boat to Djibouti. This was my first time in the boat. My mom traveled with us to Djibouti. On the boat we stay for two or three days. Once we arrived in Djibouti, we went to the hotel, and we stayed there three months to get all the paperwork done. There was a beach behind us. There were so many crabs! I got bit by some of them. If we wanted to go swimming, we could—anytime we want. After three months, it was time to go to America. My mom went back to Yemen. She didn't get a visa. In the end, only I got to go to America with my old brother, my uncle, his wife, and his kids. My mom and my sisters stayed behind in Yemen.

We went in the airplane and travelled to Istanbul, Turkey. We stayed in the airport for one whole day. It was bad because we didn't have anything to sleep on, so we just slept on the floor. We couldn't go out to a hotel because we didn't have a green card. My uncle, Abdul, and his family—Mohammed, Ganna, and Haroon all had green cards and could go out, but everybody else had just a visa. So we all stayed together in the airport. After a while, we got on another airplane and traveled to New York City. My uncle's brother came and took us to Rochester. It was very cold because it was fall. It was very, very cold to me because in Yemen it's so hot. Yemen in the winter is like America in summer. It was freezing here, and we had to wait for a long time to get our bags. They brought two cars, so we could all go. We stopped to eat Yemeni food, then we drove to Rochester.

I was a little bit sad because I was thinking America is all covered in snow. I was so excited to play in the snow and see the snow, but there was no snow because it was fall. I asked my uncle, "Is there snow?" And he told me, "Not yet." He told me, "It will come in the wintertime." When I first came to Rochester, we stayed home for two weeks. Halloween came, and my uncle told us, "If you want to go get candy, you can go out." But we didn't know what to do, so he told us, "When you go to a house you should tell them trick-or-treat, so just go." We were so excited! I was saying in my mind, "Why they give us candy?" That was my best day in America.

On the first day of school I went to East High School. It was kind of good and bad at the same time because the students were so terrible—they would always fight. I used to witness a fight like every day, and there was a lot of bullying. You would have to fight every day, if you were there. A lot of trouble—a lot, a lot of trouble. It was good because my teachers were so nice. Ms. Hoover, who taught social studies, used to stay with me after school to help me with my homework. East High School middle school teachers were so nice and kind.

Later, my family moved to Brighton. My uncle said that there are really good schools there. He found us a house to rent. They gave me a laptop—I didn't know anything about the laptop…how to open it…how to use it…I didn't know anything. In Yemen we don't have them—we never used a laptop before. In America it was different. Turned out that I couldn't do my homework because it was all on the tablet.

I asked to do eighth grade again. I wanted to stay there because it took me a long time to understand school, and I felt it would be good for me to repeat it. Now, I am in eighth grade, and I'm doing good. I understand a lot of things. I had a lot of friends at East High School that spoke Arabic. I didn't learn English because I was only speaking Arabic. I just learn bad words in English, but when I came to Brighton, there was no cursing. My teachers there were nice—Ms. Hallagan and Ms. Martinez, they are so kind. I learned new things. I also learned that I couldn't read and write because in Yemen, I couldn't go to school. Brighton helped me because all of my friends speak different languages, and we all speak English together, to one another. Brighton teachers taught me how to read and write.

Last summer, Ms. Hallagan told us we could go to a summer camp for two weeks. Camp Gorham, it was called. It was so nice, and it was for free. Only five people from the school could go—Abdul and I both got to go. The first day at camp Gorham was a little bit boring because we couldn't do anything. At first I was thinking, "Why did I come here if we are just only going to play soccer? I can play soccer at home." They told us to swim in the deep end of the lake for a swimming test. It was to see if we could go in the deep end without a life jacket.

After that first day, they told us to pick three things that we would like to do each day. I picked mountain biking, rock climbing, and swimming the first week. The second week, I picked paddle boarding, canoeing, and swimming, and rock climbing. In the evening they asked us, "What would you rather do, paddle boarding or horse riding?" To do horse riding, you have to go give the horse food, learn about the horse, and go to the horse place where they sleep." I picked paddle boarding because I like the lake. Abdul picked horse riding because he said it was too cold. We both had a good time.

The lunch was very good because you can have as much as you want. We used to always play Uno and talk. After that, we had like one hour to go and then we had to stay in the cabin. We stayed for two weeks. We slept in a cabin. It was me and Abdul, and also Fernando, Joey, Noah, Xavier and this other guy…I don't remember his name. When we had free time, we'd run and push each other to the lake—whoever would fall in, he would just lose—and whoever would lose had to clean the cabin.

When I think about Yemen, I miss my friends, my mom, and my sisters. I miss the mountains where I used to go biking…I miss that. When I was in Yemen, I was feeling free to go anywhere, but here in America I cannot go just anywhere I want.

What is my goal? I don't want to stay in one country. I wanted to go to America, but I don't want to stay in just one country. My goal is to work on something big and travel to all the countries in the world. I would like to travel everywhere, and I want to travel on a boat. If I have a free month, I want to go visit my mom. I want to go visit all of the countries like China, Japan, and Turkey. The country I want to travel the most is China. There are interesting things there. Things that I've never seen in my whole life.

greencardvoices.org/speakers/Sultan-Yahya

AFRICA
Goma,
Democratic
Republic
of the Congo

Sekuye Bolende

Born: Goma, Democratic Republic of the Congo
Current City: Buffalo, NY

"THERE CAME A DAY WHEN WE HAD TO STOP GOING TO SCHOOL BECAUSE OF THE MONEY. MY MOM'S BUSINESS WASN'T GOING REALLY GOOD. FOR SCHOOL WE HAD TO HAVE UNIFORMS, SCHOOL FEES, AND BOOKS. WE ALSO NEEDED MONEY FOR FOOD, AND IT WAS REALLY HARD FOR MY MOM TO PROVIDE FOR ALL THAT."

I was born in Goma, the capital of North Kivu province in the eastern Democratic Republic of the Congo. I don't remember much because I was really young when I was there, but I do remember the day that I had to leave with all my family—my mom, my siblings, my cousins, and my dad. On that day, I was also going to school in the morning. I remember that day was a big celebration, sort of a Christmas Eve. We had gone to visit my cousins. I didn't go with my parents—I was with my sister, uncles, and cousins. We were mostly just kids going to see them because that's what we would always do—go visit them. When we arrived, right in front of the house, we heard people singing and also some people running and also some people shouting. We saw people with guns and so we ran right away from the house. I remember the day, which was the day we had to hide ourselves. This day was a day on which my cousins...

I think I was about six years old when we had to flee to Uganda. I don't remember exactly because I was so very young. I was really nervous about going to a different country because they also speak different languages. But I was happy with the fact that my dad was there with us. At first, we came with five family members—my dad, my mom, and three kids, two sisters and me. After that, my three cousins came. My mom brought them with her to Uganda. It was kind of hard learning a new language again.

My mom used to travel and make money. My dad lived near Kampala in Uganda. My mom used to sometimes come to Kampala and then go to Goma. That's how she would make money for us to go to school. I remember when I started going to school that it was hard for my little brother to be alone in school. He needed me, and he started crying. I remember the day he started crying—he looked like he didn't want to be away from my side.

There came a day when we had to stop going to school because of the money. My mom's business wasn't going really good. For school we had to have uniforms, school fees, and books. We also needed money for food, and it was really hard for my mom to provide for all that. In Uganda I went to school, but I didn't really go that long. I only went when I was younger. It was hard for us because we were refugees. It was also hard for us seeing other kids going to school. Most of our neighbors' kids were going to school. It was only us that couldn't go, so that was hard for me. Some of our neighbors were mean and aggressive, saying we would never go to school. It was not making my mom happy seeing our kids' neighbors go to school and us not going. It was not a happy thing.

We came to America on November 4, 2016. The journey from the airport was really good. It was my first time to be on an airplane actually, and it was such a great experience for me. I was sitting with my siblings and cousins and also with my mom. When we came here there was a person waiting for us who actually really welcomed us. She was our caseworker. It was actually really good.

It was basically what I thought was the wintertime. It was beautiful because we had the leaves that were falling off the trees. It was fall, and it was cool. We couldn't really go outside a lot because it was cold at that time. We got to stay inside because we had to get ready because it takes time to go back again to school because of the process at Journey's End. Because we are a family of eight, it took time for us to get put in our separate grades and classes—they had to do that for six of us kids. The process was done by my dad, who had to work with our caseworker. All of that—the papers we had to sign—it took us time. We had to wait until the next year in January 2017 to start school.

When I arrived in America, I saw really a lot of stuff I have never seen before—especially the food. The caseworker gave every person a big box that had our names on it. Inside there were snacks and stuff like that. It was actually really crazy. We would have a big house because right now there are eight in the family. My first home…it was big. That's what I remember. We also had neighbors. At first, we thought the neighbors were good. Then we started school and we realized something was not right about them. There was a day that there was a lot of things going on with the neighbors. We found out the neighborhood we were in is not good. Things were not safe for us as kids. There was a lot of violence. One of the neighbors in the front got killed with a knife. Then some people came and started saying that the previous day someone was in the back of the house. They kept saying that he was hiding inside our house. We were like, "What?" There were people throwing stones at my house and my dad, I remember, I was sleeping and then one of my cousins came in to wake me up, and she was crying and scared.

I got enrolled in the public school #19 at first, which is a Native American magnet School. I remember that it was really hard for me and my cousins because of the language. I think I had a little bit of English in me because of Uganda. I was learning, but it was really hard for me to pronouncc words correctly and some students were laughing at us—especially if asked the teacher a question. Math was hard. It was really tough. Not having friends was really tough for me and my cousins too, but there were some students that would come up to us and some of them, they became really my best friends.

When I came to Lafayette High School, I was really nervous. Mostly because of the fact that it was high school, and people say a lot of things about high school. I missed the friends that I made in school #19, even if I had some hard times. But this time, students were coming to us, and they started talking to us. At Lafayette I found people that were speaking the same language as me. A lot of students were from different cultures, and I felt I was welcomed. I felt really good—like I had a family. I had a teacher who was my support there also. I like school, especially global studies. Last year I did cheerleading—it's fun! I like how the girls are having fun together. It's just fun, but with my dad doesn't see it as a sport, but I see it as a sport.

In the future, I want to be a nurse. It's a feeling that I just want to help. I want to be a nurse because I want to help people—especially poor kids or homeless and people who are in need. It's my dream career.

greencardvoices.org/speakers/Sekuye-Bolende

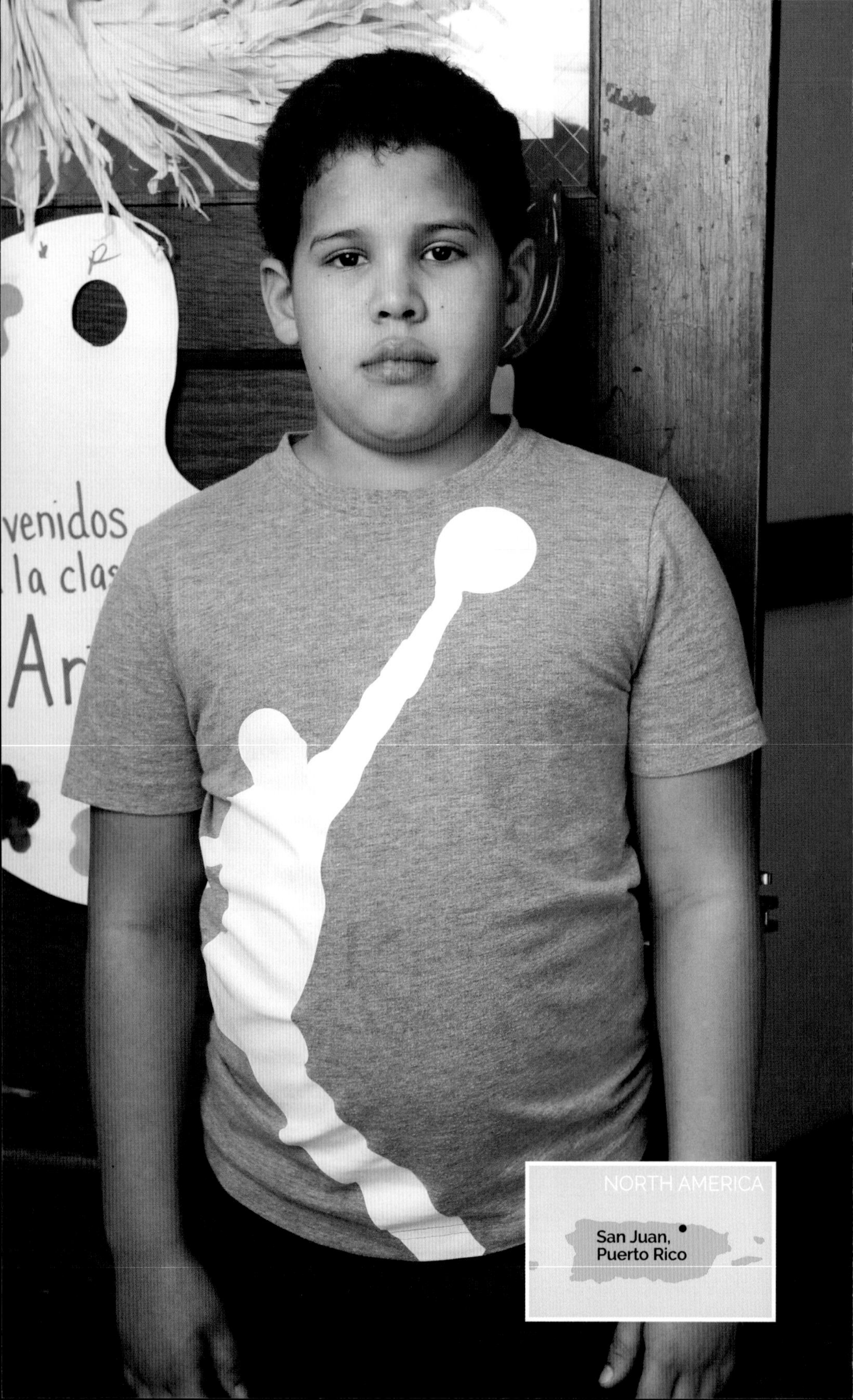

NORTH AMERICA

San Juan,
Puerto Rico

Jeffrey Omar Cruz

Born: San Juan, Puerto Rico
Current City: Rochester, NY

"THE HOUSE IS STILL BROKEN. BUT THE ELECTRICITY IS BACK IN MANY PLACES, BUT THE STREETS ARE STILL BROKEN. SO, I THINK I WILL STAY HERE. I HOPE THAT MY MOM AND MY SISTER COME AND STAY HERE, TOO."

My name is Jeffrey Omar Cruz. I'm from Manati in the northern part of Puerto Rico. I have one brother, who is here with me, and one sister, but she lives in Puerto Rico with my mom. I also have many friends in Puerto Rico. Before Hurricane Maria, life was good. I would go to school, and on the weekends, I would play with my friends, we liked to play basketball.

I stayed in Puerto Rico during the whole Hurricane Maria, from when it started, until it finished. When Maria finished, we decided that it would be hard for us to stay there. We thought about leaving. Maria was so bad—bad because Hurricane Maria took our house, and we didn't have any electricity left.

My tití said to my grandma that I needed to come and live with them in New York. My grandma said, "Good." My tití and my cousin came to Puerto Rico to get my brother and me. My mom and my sister stayed behind in Puerto Rico. I was nine years old when I left Puerto Rico. We first travelled to Florida. From Florida we went to Rochester. We only stopped in Florida on the way for three hours only. When we arrived in the airport in Rochester my tio was waiting for us as well as my grandma. There we were—me, my brother, my tití, and my cousin.

Afterwards, I went to the government office and got the paper that I needed to be able to enroll in school. My first day in school in Rochester was very good because I got new friends—now, my best friends and a new teacher. Now I live with my grandma and my brother and my tití and my cousin. I have a PlayStation and play with my brother. We ride bikes. We also go to my uncle's house and play. In school I like math—I like subtraction and addition.

In the future, I want to go to Puerto Rico to help people because life without electricity is very difficult. This past summer I went to Puerto Rico to see my mom and my sister and play with my friends. The house is still broken, but the electricity is back in many places, but the streets are still broken, so, I think I will stay here. I hope that my mom and my sister come and stay here, too. I was told that I might go to Pennsylvania because my cousin and my madrastra are there. I heard good things about it. In the future, I want to finish school, and I want to work.

greencardvoices.org/speakers/Jeffrey-Omar-Cruz

ASIA
Kyaukpyu,
Myanmar

Jonnoto Nor Ahmad

Born: Kyaukpyu, Myanmar (Rohingya)
Current City: Buffalo, NY

"I WANT TO DO SOMETHING FOR MY FATHER TO BE PROUD OF ME....MY GOAL IS THAT I WANT TO GO TO COLLEGE. I WANT TO HAVE A JOB AND BE THE ART TEACHER."

What I remember about the time when I lived in the Rohingya area was that some of the Burmese military were killing my people. I also remember that some of the mothers and fathers were being killed. Mothers and fathers were putting their sons and daughters in safe place. The military were doing the bad thing to the girls, but sometimes they were just killing the whole family. It is the Burmese military that are killing the Rohingya because they want all the areas where the Rohingya are living for themselves.

It was kind of not safe in Burma for us too. We had to leave because they were killing so many people in the Rohingya area, so we left Burma by boat. During my time in Burma, I lived through some of the most difficult times in my life. But I also have lots of good memories. The name of the place where I lived and was born is Kyaukpyu. It's a very pretty place, really beautiful. It's made up of many businesses like fishing, rice farming, and trade. There is the Indian Ocean with such a beautiful harbor. We spent a lot of good times in the ocean when I was young. I remember that we went swimming in the ocean.

I also didn't understand the Burmese language. Among the Rohingya, some of us speak the Burmese language, but some of us do not. I learned only a little bit. I attended the Burmese school. One day when I came home from Burmese school, my parents talked to my grandma and decided that my sister and I would be going to Malaysia. I would feel so lonely, if my sister went alone. I wanted to go with my sister, so I went with her to Malaysia.

So many people loved and cared about me in Kyaukpyu—an auntie, uncle, also my whole neighborhood. There is so much love I remember that and the people. After we left Burma and went to Malaysia, my other family members, like my auntie and uncle, they came to Malaysia, too. In Malaysia some of them lived with us. Eventually most of my extended family was in Malaysia after leaving the Rohingya area.

I was twelve or thirteen years old when I moved to Malaysia. But once we arrived, I didn't have any school because I'm not a citizen. My father decided to come to America because he wants for his daughters and sons to have education because he has had too long of a time with no education. My father said he will try and have us go to the U.S.

I was in Malaysia for three years. I took care of my family. I took care of my young brother. I helped my mom with the housework, like cooking. I was still not attending school because if I didn't have citizenship there and because the place I lived was far away from the school. I really missed the school. My cousin said that the school is important, and so I asked him, "Why am I missing my Burmese school? Why did I come to Malaysia?" It was so hard because we didn't have the chance to go to school, but, on the other hand, Malaysia was safer for me.

When my parents explained to me that we are going to the .S. I was very sad because it was just another new place. I told my mom that I would not go, that we cannot go, but I had to follow my father. I respect him, so I went. I felt really nervous. I thought, "How is my life going to be? I was going to the U.S.?!" The first day that I went to the U.S. I was feeling very nervous, but later it got better.

I have had the medical checkup so many times. They had so many questions for me. I had some problems because some of the information was wrong—they confused the age of me and my sister on the documents. It made us late coming to the U.S. because they had to fix the documents. I remember the day I left because my auntie and uncle came to our home and helped with packing the clothes. We were reading from the list, and they just helped us to pack. They are so amazing, but they had to leave us before we went to the airport. They could not come with us.

During the journey I do not remember very much because that day my head was so dizzy. I could not even open up my eyes. I just closed my eyes and kept sleeping. When we arrived in Buffalo, we had to look for our luggage and wait for the caseworker. He had a problem meeting us because we don't know who he is and how he looks. We also had a hard time when we got there because the caseworker did not find my father's friend's house. He was supposed to put our things at my father's friend's house, but he put them at some other place. We had to wait one month for our things because the caseworker could not find the right house for us to live in.

During the first week in America I had a hard time sleeping, and I was not sleeping at night. I was very sad to remember my family members—my auntie and uncle—so I felt like I wanted to go back to Malaysia. I also saw that some of the kids were going to school, and I was really happy about that. But I was also scared. I thought about how I didn't know how to speak English. I thought it would be difficult with the English speaking, but I really wanted to go to school.

I have two sisters and two brothers. My two brothers are still so young, and my sister is the oldest. She attended the Newcomers Academy here in Buffalo, but she couldn't make it and didn't attend anymore school. She left and got married. Now, she is going to be a mother. She lives with us in my house with me, my parents, and my little brothers.

When I arrived, it was in the middle of the school year in 2016. I went to the school PS #94 West Hertel Academy here in Buffalo. Some of the students helped me. Most of the African girls, they were my friends in School 94. One girl especially was helping me. I really appreciated it. She is a really good girl. Anything, anything I didn't know, I would ask her. Some of them could not help because they have to work, but the African girls really helped. Also, the English teacher helped me with my English. She helped with speaking and writing. I knew a little bit of English before I came to America because I researched a little bit about the English. I knew I would need the English, so I talked to my friend in English to practice. The more I talked, the more I could speak, and that's how I learned.

Now I go to Lafayette International High School. I'm really happy here. The life here is good because some of the teachers really helped me with what I needed. A lot of teachers helped me because I didn't understand any of the classwork because it was in English, but my teachers made it easier for me. I'm really happy when I help someone else. In Business class, Global class, and Algebra class I help other students. I have learned more English, too. My favorite subjects are Algebra, Global Studies, Art, and Biology. After school, I listen to the teacher and that's how I am preparing for the exam. On the weekends, I just stay home and look at some of the exam papers and review. I also have to look or care for my other cousin and my little brothers.

I was not really going outside when I first came here. I really felt uncomfortable. Everything was so different. I would just stay home all day. But one time I went to Niagara Falls. It was so beautiful. That day that we went to

Niagara Falls, my father was upset with me. He wanted me to go outside, but I didn't want to go. He said to me, "If you are not going, I will be angry with you." So, I followed him so that I wouldn't get in trouble. When I got there, I saw it was so beautiful.

For goals, I would like to go to college. I want to do something for my father to be proud of me. I am thinking I am going to be an art teacher. I like art. When I had depression, I was going to the art class and drawing, and now my depression is gone. I enjoy painting most. I'm still learning from Ms. Lipsitz—she is the teacher. She said, "You should come to the art club." I often go there and learn from her. I paint different things—the portrait, the landscape. The teacher sometimes wants us to draw our home country or a landscape from there or here. I hope my father is really proud of me.

I miss my grandma—she is still in Burma. I really hope one day I can go back to Burma to meet with my grandma and my cousins, but I am happy to live here because I get a better education. My goal is that I want to go to college. I want to have a job and be the art teacher. I want to become a U.S. citizen. Then, I want to go to Burma, see my cousin and my grandma and see how they are living. After, I want to go around to look at the world.

greencardvoices.org/speakers/Jonnoto-Nor-Ahmad

EUROPE
Kastoria,
Greece

Stela Ciko

Born: Kastoria, Greece (Albanian) **Raised:** Korçë, Albania
Current City: Rochester, NY

"I THINK IT'S VERY IMPORTANT THAT ALL IMMIGRANTS REMEMBER THEIR ORIGINS, BUT ALSO WHO THEY ARE AND WHAT OPPORTUNITIES THEY HAVE IN FRONT OF THEM."

I was born in Kastoria in Northern Greece, close to Albanian border. My parents moved there because there was a war in Albania in the 1990s. They moved there for safety, stability, economic reasons, and just life in general. Then by the time I was born, we moved back to Albania to the town of Korçë. It was on the other side of the border, just forty miles away from Kastoria. There, I grew up with my parents and sisters.

We had family in both Greece and Albania, and also in America. We had a glorified image of America and because of that we all wanted to come here. Not just my family, but all our other relatives too. Albania wasn't really a great place for a person to get good education, go to college, and end up with a good job after. School was very important to all of us. When I ask my mom now why we moved here, she says, "When I thought about what you kids would do after middle school, I didn't know what to think because there was nothing else for you there. There was nowhere for us to go."

Public education in Albania wasn't very good. Private schools were a much better option for the educational system, so my parents decided to put my sisters and I into a private Greek school that held classes in Greek, Albanian, and English. Students there learned all three languages. My parents had to pay a fee every month. Because many parents would run out of money, my classmates would have to leave the private school and enroll back to public school. When I was young, I couldn't understand why their parents wouldn't want them to be in a better school, but then I realized that they just couldn't afford to pay for their children's education. We had to stay on top of our homework. Our mom helped us a lot with that. When we were young, she would stay on top of us to make sure that we did all our homework and everything we needed to do for school. She also made sure that we were good people and that we presented ourselves as kind and good to others.

In Albania, conditions of life weren't really that great. There was running water but not hot water. When you wanted to shower, you had to wait for the boiler to finish heating the water, and there was not enough hot water for everyone in the family. So if you were living in a big family, for example, you had to think about that and not use up all the hot water—leave some for others. The roads were narrow, muddy, and full of potholes. In winters, we wouldn't have good quality shoes that prevented snow or water from getting into them. We would wear plastic bags on top of two to three layers of socks, and then put our feet into boots. Then we could walk to our bus stop and go to school.

My parents had in mind to move either to Germany or some place in Western Europe or to America through the green card lottery. Both of my parents applied every year in hopes to get in. They had to go through a whole procedure of filling out applications. Finally, my mom won it in 2014! My mom's cousin, who helped us all fill out the applications, called home and said, "You're a winner!" But my mom just couldn't believe him. He had to come over to our house and show her the computer page. It said her first name, last name, and "you won the lottery!" It was a whole celebration for all of us. It's a huge feat to actually win the lottery. After winning it and coming here, we could attend a good college and then finally get good jobs.

In Albania, I was comfortable because I always went to school with the same people from kindergarten through middle school. I didn't have to think about what I said or who I hung out with. But once I got here, I had to think about what to say and how to start small talk with limited English. The cultural aspect was difficult too—not just the language. The way you talk with someone in Albania is different than in America. I couldn't make friends here as easily as I could if I was there.

Packing was a tough challenge for my mom and my dad since they had to pack their entire life's belongings. They had to decide what to take and what to leave behind. They had to consider the limited amount of space. We had ten big fifty-pound luggage bags, two per person that we took to the airport. We had stuffed anything in there that we could that was useful. None of us knew English well. My sisters and I only had a fifth-grade level of English. We had to help the whole family get around the airport by asking basic questions. I remember, it's kind of a funny story, but when we had to go from the top floor to the bottom floor to get to our flight, we didn't know where the elevators were…

and we had ten big pieces of luggage. We decided we were going to take the escalator. We stacked the luggage up on top of each other. It's only funny because the luggage started rolling over and fell all the way down. A security person had to come over and show us where the elevator was.

When we arrived in Rochester, it was midnight, so I couldn't really see much. From my phone conversations with my uncle, America seemed like a very big place—open and lively. But when I came here, I found out that in the suburbs it's very quiet. Homes have a whole lawn in front of them, and they're spaced out from their neighbors, so it's very different from city life. It took my sisters and me a while to get used to that. After arriving here, we had a choice of what middle school to attend. My uncle researched which districts were the top two in the area we lived. One day my dad took my sisters and I out for a car ride and showed us both schools. After seeing both of them, we chose the one that was nearest a plaza with food, so we could be around more people. My parents found an apartment in that district, and we started going there.

At first, it was challenging because the school district was very advanced. The standard of education was high, and the school really well-organized. We had to deal with classes that were maybe a little more advanced than in Albania. On top of that, we still had to learn English. Once I got the hang of it, I started advancing through classes, taking honors classes. The sole fact that America offered honors classes tells you that this is where you want to be for your education. Once I started learning English better, I became good friends with other immigrants and also American people. This opened my eyes to other peoples' stories and also to Americans and how they viewed their life here.

In high school, I started to really think about my life and that I was an immigrant. I realized that I actually had a second chance of reliving my whole life, basically from scratch. I decided that I was going to stop focusing on learning how to live like an American. I would start living like I would live in Albania or Greece. I started going back to all my hobbies that I had before. I started dance and volleyball, which I had disregarded at first when I came here because I was so focused on learning English and being a good American.

Now my main focus in life is getting good grades and getting into a good college. My goal is to get a good job that pays enough that I don't ever have to worry about my economic status. If I have a need or my parents have a need, I can provide for it. Reaching this goal would help fulfill the whole reason why my parents sacrificed everything they had. In America, I can reach my potential. I would not have the chance to do this if I was in another place other than here.

I think it's very important that all immigrants remember their origins, but also who they are and what opportunities they have in front of them. Even if they're not the smartest or the most talkative, they can always find something and take the chance to be the best version of themselves. They can live a life where they do not have to worry. They can just be happy. Immigrants might have a need or desire to express, "Oh, I'm an immigrant" to provide an excuse to feel better. Immigrants should remember that even if they feel like an outsider in the beginning, by pushing through and not getting caught up in their struggles, they can move forward to fulfill whatever they can. That's the best thing we, immigrants, can do for ourselves.

greencardvoices.org/speakers/Stela-Ciko

AFRICA

Gitega,
Burundi

Ca Arrive Rushikana

Born: Gitega, Burundi
Current City: Buffalo, NY

"HERE IN SCHOOL IN AMERICA, WE GOT SOME TECHNOLOGY, BUT BACK IN THE DAY IN AFRICA, WE DID NOT HAVE ANY TECHNOLOGY. WE ONLY USED A PEN TO WRITE ON PAPER."

I was born in Burundi, but my father was born in Congo. I used to live with my grandma, grandpa, my mom, my brothers, and my sisters. There were three adults in my house. My grandparents still live in that house—the place that my grandparents have is beautiful. My grandma is blessed. I did not like the idea to live in a refugee camp because I had to go and live with my mom only. My dad just left us when I was about three years. He went to Zambia with my uncle.

I lived with my mom for three years, then it was decided that I was to move with my dad's brother who lived in the capital city, Gitega. I lived with my uncle, my dad's brother, for five years. When I was nine or ten years old, I went to live with my father's sister and my other uncle and their two kids. My uncle had two wives—his wife and the wife he loved named Vesty. Vesty had one baby. After five years living with my aunt, we decided that I would live with my dad's brother again for two years. So I went back to live with him. I lived with aunties and uncles my whole life—I did not live with my mom.

My dad, who lived in Zambia decided to move to America. He moved to America and lived there for twelve years. My dad came first to America when I was living with my auntie, his sister. He had married his new wife in Zambia—he loves her. She had two babies in Zambia. They all moved together to America. My uncle and auntie, their kids, my sister, my brothers, and I came to America to be with my father. Another sister also came, but she came by herself because she already was eighteen years old. I'm about to have a two-year anniversary since my arrival in America. I came in 2018.

It was 2014, and my aunt that I was living with decided that she wanted to go to America. My dad was calling her and asking her to come. She said, "Let's go!" My dad said to her, "This country is good. Join us." So, my auntie, she just said, "Yes!" but she was a little bit scared. I knew that she was scared because she did not know how it would be living in another country. She had lived in another country before, but that was long time ago.

I was confused, and I was also excited because I did not know where we would be going. At that point, there was like thirteen of us in the house—my uncle and my auntie, my cousins and brothers and sisters. That's how we lived. I cared for my little brother. When my dad left us, I was three years old, and my mom was pregnant at the time with my little brother; he is the youngest.

When I lived in Burundi, I went to school. The school was a free school, but it was not a good school. It was just a school to go to and start learning to read and do some other work. In that school you can't use the calculator, you had to use your brain. The teachers were the only people using the calculators. We didn't have all the human rights because the education was not assured for you. It was not decided by you who can go study. Sometimes they would tell you to stay in one place, and you couldn't move to the next grade. You only had three minutes to take a break. I also just didn't know how to study—no one explained much. There were no books, no computers—you could not ask questions. Here in school in America, we got some technology, but back in the day in Africa, we did not have any technology. We only used a pen to write on paper. Some students even didn't have paper, and if you don't have paper, you have go to and borrow it from the teacher. They just gave it to you—a little piece of it so you can write.

When I came to America, I was excited to see my dad again because I had ten years without seeing my dad. That's why it was exciting. I traveled with my aunt, not with my mom with my dad. We flew from Burundi to Ethiopia, then we changed to the big plane and took another one after that. We parked in France, and from there we went to Washington, D.C. Then, we took another plane to right to Buffalo.

The final stop was in Buffalo, and I was excited just to see my dad. He was waiting for me. He had four more kids, and he was already married to his new wife when he came to America. With her he had two kids before he moved to America, and two kids after he moved here. When we came to America, it was special to see my father. At the airport, there was my father and his friends and my stepmom. He just gave me hug, and we talked about the time back in the day. He told me the whole story—how he decided to move to Zambia and after that to America, and why he decided to leave me and with my mom and my grandma. We were celebrating him seeing me again by sitting, talking and eating.

On the first day or in the first week really, we took time to sit down and talk, drink some water and tell our stories. I told my dad told how we moved, what our life was like, and that life there was difficult. My dad told me how his life was in Zambia—they lived in a refugee camp. It was not how they were living in America; it was different there. Sometimes they could not wear fresh, clean clothes for whole week because the water was too far away. When I first got there, we were sitting in his house, chilling and relaxing and talking about African things. We spoke French—I like to speak French. I was watching French movies. At that point, I didn't speak or understand any English, so my dad also forced me to watch some videos of the people speaking in English. Back then I did not like it or focus on that too much, but now, I thank him for this.

My life now is good. I'm going to school. When I come back from school, I do my homework. I just got piano at home because I learned how to play piano for four years when I was in Africa. When I just get home, and I don't have anything to do, I just try to play piano. After piano, I do math. I like math class. It is my favorite class.

In the future, I just want to be like big artist with paintings on the street. They are called murals—the ones that you see when you go to downtown. I just want make art that is on the side of the buildings or houses. We have some great art right here in Buffalo. Some of the art is sometimes a little crazy—sometimes you can just go walking and you will find people that draw. They draw down near the river in a place called Buffalo River Works. It's located along the banks of the Buffalo River. So in the future, I just want draw on a side of the house and make big art. My goal is to be a big artist someday.

greencardvoices.org/speakers/Ca-Arrive-Rushikana

NORTH AMERICA

Penuelas,
Puerto Rico

Wanlee Arys Irizarry Pacheco

Born: Penuelas, Puerto Rico
Current City: Rochester, NY

"THE HURRICANE MARIA IS OVER, BUT LIFE IS NO GOOD. THERE IS NO WATER, NO FOOD, AND NO ELECTRICITY."

I am from Penuelas, Puerto Rico. It's in the southern part of the island, near Ponce. I lived there with my mother, father, brother and five dogs. Before the Hurricane Maria came to my town, the town was clean with tall trees. It was a good place to live.

My grandma gave us the notice that the hurricane was coming. It came at night. When I woke up there was no electricity in the whole town. My dad and my mom were sleeping, and my brother and I woke up my father. He said, "We are going to the house of your grandma because there are no trees nearby, and it's more safe." I got all my dogs, and we went there. When I got there, my grandma was very nervous and scared. I heard her crying. I see that I'm feeling very sad and nervous too. My family house is in the mountains, so it was not safe. When the hurricane came, the trees started falling down, metal was going in the air, and there was so, so much rain, and so much wind. The dogs were frightened—they were so scared.

When the Hurricane Maria was over, I saw my grandma's tree in the window of her neighbor's house. I went to check my house. When I opened the door of my house, there was so much water. I saw the trees on the floor. I saw metal in there. I saw so much destroyed, but my family is okay. My parents were in the house with my grandma. They were okay. My dogs were in the house of my grandma, and they were okay.

The Hurricane Maria is over, but life is no good. There is no water, no food, and no electricity. Me, I would go with my mother to get supplies. I go to buy water and food, but the money is not enough. The water in the shop are so costly. When I buy the water, it is only one bottle to a person—one to a person! We only can buy one for each person. That is not enough water for us. Later FEMA brought us water and Army food.

My mom said she wanted a new life and to move to Rochester because we have family there. That is why we came here. To be on an airplane it was my dream. I like airplanes—they are so beautiful. When I started the school in here in Rochester, I feel so nervous when I go to my first class. I got lost. One of the girls saw that I was lost, and she helped me. My uncle helped me to get to my class. When I walked to the classroom, I feel bad. I felt shy because I'm new. It's was so strange…more teachers, more strangers, strange things.

Now I like the school. I have so many friends, and I like the English class. I'm so happy to come here, and I'm so happy to be able to stay here. On the weekend I play with my brother, text with my friends, and play Fortnite… not much else.

In the future, I want to study policing. I want to work for the FBI. I want to go to Puerto Rico and see my friends there. One day I want to buy a house. I want to work, and I want a family.

greencardvoices.org/speakers/Wanlee-Arys-Irizarry-Pacheco

ENGLISH LITERATURE
GARNETT
ENGLISH LITERATURE
GARNETT
THE HOME BOOK OF VERSE
AMERICAN IDEALS
AFRICA
Kibuye,
Rwanda

Flavia Kayitesi

Born: Kibuye, Rwanda
Current City: Buffalo, NY

"EDUCATION WAS NOT GOOD THERE—THEY NEVER FED US NOR GAVE US A BOOK OR PEN. WE WOULD JUST GO TO SCHOOL, AND WE WOULD HAVE TO PAY MONEY TO BUY BOOKS—WE HAD TO PAY MONEY FOR SCHOOL LUNCH, FOR SCHOOL CLOTHES..."

I remember many things in Rwanda. I remember how I used to play with my sisters, my friends, and my neighbors, but life was not easy. Life was very difficult because there was no water in Camp. There was not enough food to eat, and my siblings used to be sick all the time because of drinking water that is not clean. I don't remember all things in Rwanda because I was very young, but I do remember that we had to go get water from so far away and that I was always tired and always sick. We had to carry the water on our head.

The Camp where we lived had many refugees, and there were only people from Congo living there. Our home was very small. The Camp was run by the UNHCR, and they would help people. They would give us food every month. During the week I would go to school. On the weekends, I would wake up in the morning, clean the house, wash dishes, and help my parents by fetching water. I did go to school, but it was not easy. Education was not good there—they never fed us nor gave us a book or pen. We would just go to school, and we would have to pay money to buy books—we had to pay money for school lunch, for school clothes…for everything. It was hard for me to go to school because life was not easy. We could not find money to buy a book. Sometimes I even didn't go to school because my parents didn't have money to buy a book or pen, so there was nothing for me to do other than listen. The teachers would just go and help other students who had money because the students who could give them a little money.

Some people were able to get out of the refugee Camp and earn some extra money, but that was very hard to do because we were not allowed to do so. We are nine children in our family—five sisters and four brothers. My parents' oldest child is my brother, and he is thirty years old and has a family of his own. My youngest little sister is ten years old. My parents have too many children and not enough money to help us all.

My parents told me that there was war in Congo. My father told me that some people came to their house and burned it. They killed all their fathers, their mothers, their sisters, and all their siblings. They killed everyone in his family, except for my father who is the only one who survived. They just came to his house and killed everybody in the house. My father told me that he was hiding under the bed, so they didn't see him. If they saw him, they would kill him too.

My mother told me that her mother died when she was fifteen years old. She has one big sister, who helped a lot after her mother passed. Their father also died, so her parents both died when she was young. She didn't have any other silbings, so my mom and her sister just came to the Camp because they didn't have any other place to live in Congo. Because everybody there, everybody, was dead. They didn't have anyone, so they just went to find a safe place and tried to find people to help them. They did say that some people took them to the big house in Kibuye where everyone was an orphan. They stayed there until they were twenty years old. After that, they had to move to the Kiziba Refugee Camp. Once my mother moved to the Refugee Camp, she met my father and they got married. My parents told me that before I was born, life was not easy. It was very difficult, especially to find food to eat. It was not easy. My mother told me that before she met my father, her older sister used to help her buy clothes and help out with everything.

Our life in the Camp was difficult. The only food we ate was rice, beans and fufu—mostly fufu and beans. My mother told me that one day they were trying to go outside of the Camp to find some food, but the police caught them and asked who they were. They answered that they are refugees from the Camp. The police told them that because they were refugees, they were not allowed to go outside of the Camp. My parents told them that they were going to look for work because their children were hungry, but the police told them that they have to go back to the Camp because they didn't have written permission to go to the city. The police told them that they had no right to look for a job, get clean water, nor search for a good place to live. On some other occasions, when it was safe, they would let refugees leave the Camp to go find food and come back. Sometimes police would not let refugees outside of Camp, especially if there is something going on in the city, or it was not safe. If the police saw that you left the Camp, they took you to the jail. Life was not easy.

I remember one day the immigration people came to our place in the refugee Camp. I was sleeping at the time. They told my parents that we were going to move to America. I was so excited. I couldn't even believe it. I thought they were lying because I never believed that I would have a good life, a good education, and live in a good house. I didn't believe it. The people told them that in a few days we will be moving to the United States. I was crying because I felt nervous. I was crying and could not stop. They told my parents that we have to do the process, and there was a long list, but in a few days we can go to America. They told my parents they were chosen because they don't have any siblings. They told them when we come to America we will find friends—other neighbors—and make a new life for ourselves…a good life…so that way we can survive. Over the next few days, we went to do the interview. We went to see a doctor, and he did a check to see if we were healthy. We had to do many processes, but after that, they took us to the airport.

The journey, for me, was good because my brothers and sisters were with me. We took three flights. We landed first in Belgium, then in New York City, and then in Buffalo. Oh my God—it was good but kind of scary! They gave us food that I didn't even know existed—it was a kind of pizza. I didn't eat anything on the airplane. I was very hungry, but I drank water only. It was my first time to see that kind of food. I was sitting with a man, but he was nice. Because I didn't understand what different things were, he was explaining it to me, but I didn't understand him, and I sometimes thought he was saying something bad, so I didn't pay attention to him. I was hungry and tired the whole time while we were on the airplane.

My older brother came in 2017, and we came in 2018. When I landed in Buffalo, I saw my brother and his family. I was missing them so much. When I came to America, I was so scared because it was my first time to come to the United States. But I was happy to see my brother, our caseworkers, and our friend. I saw many buildings, many cars. It was my first time actually seeing many cars in the street. It was my first time seeing many people—Black people and White people mixing together. I was so happy seeing Black people and White people talking in other languages that I don't speak. I was so happy!

I was fifteen years old when I came to the U.S. in 2018. In the first week when I came to Buffalo, I was just in our house, sitting, because we didn't have a TV or phone. I was sitting with my sisters talking about how life is going to be in America. Everything was different. Back in Africa, we used to play outside with our friends in the compound and eat together, but when we came here,

I saw everything change. I had to stay in the house—not go anywhere—because I didn't know everyone. I was always looking outside the window, and I didn't see anybody walking outside. I was like, "What happened here? There is nobody outside playing around." But my big sister told me that that's how we live—if you want to play, you can go to the park or play with your sister.

I was always staying in the house eating and drinking because we had many foods in the fridge. Pizza—it tasted very different—it was my first time that I ate pizza. Oh my God, my sister told me that I should try it. It tasted good, but I was scared. I thought, "You want to kill me?" I never ate anything like this thing before! Because when I first tasted pizza on the plane, it was not good. Then I always ate pizza with my sisters, and I really liked it.

In my country, I used to eat fufu and beans every day. But here we eat breakfast, lunch, dinner, and many other kinds of food—different foods. I tasted chicken—it was not my first time, but it was my first time eating chicken two times in a week! I was so happy because it was my first time having many foods around. I was happy watching my sisters happy and not be sick. If they got sick, they could go to the doctor, and they would help them. I was very happy.

I came to America on March 13. In the first week, my brothers took me to Niagara Falls. I was like, "Oh my God, this place is beautiful!" It was my first time going out with my brothers in a car! They took me also to the downtown to see the tall buildings and to see the houses. I was so happy. They took me somewhere else in a different village, and there we visited my old friend from the Camp. In the first week, our caseworker always took us to the market and helped us buy food and things to clean the house with. It was my first-time shopping in America, so she helped us.

My caseworker, she took me to this school at Lafayette. She took me here because I was scared. Everyone was speaking a different language. I was like, "I want to go back to my country because I cannot live in this country where everyone speaks their own language. I don't understand what they are saying." Even though they were not talking about me, I felt nervous because I thought they were talking about me. I came here to study in ninth grade, but because my English was so bad, I had to repeat the ninth grade. It was good that I did because education is very different here. Education…food…clothes…everything is different. I wear shoes here. Going to school here was very difficult and very different from Rwanda.

I used to always cry. I missed my friends, and I missed how we play. I miss the culture, how my friend used to tell me stories. During the night, we used to sit down in the house, talking, and eat yam together. I used to miss that. Now I really like this place, I have many things that I like and want. For the subjects, I like biology, global studies and math. Before I didn't like math because it was difficult for me. But now I like math. Sometimes I stay after school, but sometimes I just take my homework home, and then do it at home. I really like this school. I am in tenth grade now.

On the weekends, I wake up at 10:00 a.m. in the morning. I then clean the house, wash dishes, watch TV, talk to my friend, and do my homework. Sometimes I read a book but not always. I like to watch Nigerian movies. Something I like is watching comedy. I watch news also to see if something is going on outside of the country like in Rwanda, if there is war there, or in Congo.

When my parents came here, it was not easy for them to find a job. First, they went to learn English for five months. Soon after they got work, my mom got sick, and she stopped going to work because her back always hurt. My dad works. My siblings all go to school—they have good education. When I was young, I used to think that I would like to be a doctor because of life that was going on in Rwanda. Many people were always sick, and I just feel like I wanted to help them have a better life. So, I want to be a doctor. If I don't change my mind, I think I will be a doctor.

I have many friends in the Camp, and we talk sometimes. They ask me how life is in America. I used to tell them that life is very good. I tell them, "If you get a chance to come here, you will like it…you will really like it." Everything changed for me, everything changed. In Rwanda, I used to sleep on the floor because there was no mattress to sleep on. Here, I have a house—I have a bed, food, good education…everything changed for me here. I have everything now.

greencardvoices.org/speakers/Flavia-Kayitesi

NORTH AMERICA

Guaynabo,
Puerto Rico

Zadquiel Jose Ortiz Lopez

Born: Guaynabo, Puerto Rico
Current City: Rochester, NY

"SEPTEMBER 20, 2017, WE HAD HURRICANE MARIA. EVERYBODY WAS SAD BECAUSE THE HOUSE CRACKED—LOTS OF WATER CAME BECAUSE HURRICANE MARIA IS A 'NUMBER FOUR' HURRICANE—IT WAS VERY STRONG."

My name is Zadquiel Jose Ortiz Lopez, and I'm from Guaynabo, which is in the northern part of Puerto Rico. My life in Puerto Rico was good. I lived with my sister, my dad, and my mom. I played basketball with my friends. I played soccer everyday.

September 20, 2017, we had Hurricane Maria. Everybody was sad because the house cracked—lots of water came because Hurricane Maria is a "number four" hurricane—it was very strong. The hurricane moved our car. The trees cracked. The roof of the house was gone. In Guaynabo, the hurricane made a lot of landslides…a lot of damage.

We left Puerto Rico because of Hurricane Maria. My madrina told me I was moving from Puerto Rico. I was sad because I would not see my friends, my grandma, and my grandfather. My grandma is sad because I was living next door, and I saw them every day. On the day we left Puerto Rico, we first were going to Florida, my sister and my mom and me. We went to Florida because my madrina said to my mom, "I can help you". I left Puerto Rico on July 28, 2018. I lived in Florida with my madrina. I have new friends. The Orlando school was good, and the teachers were good. In the park the people talk in English, and I don't know English. In Florida everybody speaks English. I lived eight months in Florida.

Then I moved to Rochester, New York because in Orlando, Florida everything was expensive. Rochester has many more streets. Here I have new friends, new teachers, and a new school. The big difference is the people talk English and in Puerto Rico everyone talks in Spanish, so it's not good for me. It's not easy to learn English.

Last year I don't speak English, and this year I learn English. I talk

English a little bit in Orlando. I am in the Rochester school now, and I'm going to learn even more English. On weekends I play PlayStation and sleep and play outside with friends. I like playing basketball and volleyball. In school math class is my favorite.

In my future, I want to help communities in Venezuela and Haiti because I like them. I like to help people and the community. I want to help the community in Venezuela and Haiti because these people have nothing. I think they don't have enough food. In Venezuela the people in power have everything but the regular people don't even have so much food.

greencardvoices.org/speakers/Zadquiel-Jose-Ortiz-Lopez

NIKE

EUROPE
Korçë,
Albania

Stivia Jorgji

Born: Korçë, Albania
Current City: Rochester, NY

"LEAVING YOUR HOME IS HARD, ESPECIALLY WHEN YOU HAVE A GOOD LIFE. SOME PEOPLE ARE NOT IN GOOD SHAPE ECONOMICALLY, AND THEY WANT TO GO TO HAVE MORE MONEY, BUT THAT WAS NOT US. WE WERE IN REALLY GOOD SHAPE, BUT WE LEFT."

My life in Albania was very, very social. I had a lot of friends, and I used to go out every day with my friends. On summer nights, sometimes we would even stay out past midnight because our houses were really close, so we were allowed to, and we would just play games and do different activities. It was really fun. We would hang out at each other's houses. I would play with my cousins and my grandparents and with my cats.

Leaving your home is hard, especially when you have a good life. Some people are not in good shape economically, and they want to go to have more money, but that was not us. We were in really good shape, but we left.
The schools there are not good. The teachers after fifth grade just kind of stop teaching. Sixth grade teachers teach all different subjects, but they don't give homework, and they just don't care. My mom was an elementary school teacher, and she knew how the schools were and she wanted to give my brother and I a good education. Also, there are no good doctors, in case you got really sick. Those were the main reasons why we left.

My mom told me that when she told my dad about our chance to go to America, my dad didn't want to go. Both my parents were teachers, and we were living a really good life. He told my mom to just throw the papers out and to not tell me and my brother, but my mom kept the documents hidden for like a month or two and then she talked to my dad again. My dad didn't really think about it at first, but then he changed his mind because he actually started thinking about the situation.

I found out that we will be moving to America in June 2016. I was really shocked because I didn't expect it to really happen. I wasn't expecting it, and my parents said, “This is the situation. What do you think about it?” I was scared. I didn’t know what to say. I was really nervous and excited but also sad because I was going to leave my family, my friends, and my cats. We finally came here May 8, 2017.

I started thinking about our trip weeks before it happened. I was really scared. When the day finally came, I was really sad. All my friends and my family were really sad. The day came and we had to first travel from Albania to Greece because we flew out of the airport in Greece. It was a really stressful trip because we had never been on a plane before, so it was our first flight. We didn’t really know how airports worked, so it was really hard, but we got through it somehow. When we arrived in Rochester, my mom’s best friend was waiting for us. I didn’t know them, so I was a little nervous. Then I just started talking to them and being friends with them. They are like my family now—we are very close.

The first year in Rochester was really hard. Especially hard were the first couple of months of school because I didn’t have any friends. No one talked to me, and I’m the type of person that doesn’t get friends easily without knowing them well. That was really hard for me because I like to be social. Even though I thought I knew English, I actually didn’t. Trying to understand what people were saying was very challenging. The one person who really helped and supported me through that hard time was my best friend. She was really the one to help me learn the English language. I learned the language the most when I was with my friends.

The past three years have been hard. It has been really, really hard. I miss my country, my family, but I’m getting used to it. It’s easier than it was before. I mostly hang out with my friends…my best friends…and my family members. We do different activities on the weekends especially because during the week we don’t have much time, but we do hang out. We go to the mall or restaurants.

In the future I want to be a doctor, either a pediatrician or an ophthalmologist. I want to have a good job, live somewhere in a big city where it’s warm, and have a family of my own. I still visit Albania every summer.
because I was gonna leave my family, my friends, and my cats. We finally came here May 8th, 2017.

I started thinking about our trip weeks before it happened. I was really scared. When the finally day came, I was really sad. All my friends, my family were really sad. The day came and we had to first travel from Albania to Greece because we flew out of the airport in Greece. It was a really stressful trip because we had never been on a plane before, so it was our first flight. We didn't really know how airports worked. So, it was really hard, but we got through it somehow. When we arrived in Rochester, my mom's best friend was waiting for us. I didn't know them so I was a little nervous. Then I just started talking to them and being friends with them. They are like my family now, we are very close.

The first year in Rochester was really hard. Especially hard were the first couple of months of school, because I didn't have any friends. No one talked to me and I'm the type of person that doesn't get friends easily without knowing them well. That was really hard for me because I like to be social. Even though I thought I knew English, I actually didn't. Trying to understand what people were saying was very challenging. The one person who really helped and supported me through that hard time was my best friend. She was really the one to help me learn the English language. I learned the language the most when I was with my friends.

It was really, really hard and the past three years have been hard. I miss my country, my family, but I'm getting used to it. It's easier than it was before. I mostly hang out with my friends, my best friends, and my family members. We do different activities, on the weekends, especially, because during the week we don't have much time. But, we do hang out, we go to the mall or restaurants.

In the future I want to be a doctor, either a pediatrician or an opthamologist. I want to have a good job, live somewhere in a big city where it's warm, and have a family of my own. I still visit Albania every summer.

greencardvoices.org/speakers/Stivia-Jorgji

Afterword

Learning from the students' stories featured in this book is just the beginning. The more important work starts when we engage in the difficult, essential, and brave conversations about the changing face of our nation.

Immigration plays a significant role in modern America—and our work seeks to build bridges that facilitate rich conversations and understanding. Consider, one in five Americans speak a language other than English at home—what a powerful opportunity for new connections and cultural growth! From classrooms to book clubs, from the individual interested in learning more about his immigrant neighbor to the business owner looking to understand her employees and business partners, this book is an important resource for all Americans.

This collection also includes a selection from our ***Act4Change*** study guide. *Act4Change* is an experiential learning tool promoting further participation among readers through scaffolded and thoughtful discussion questions and activities focused on hands-on learning. Each activity emphasizes personal growth and knowledge acquisition. The goal is to help teachers, students, and those experiencing our multimedia publications to more closely examine their own stories, while learning about the lives of others.

You can also further engage with your communities and learn more about contemporary immigration through ***Story Stitch***, a card-based guided storytelling activity which connects individuals across different backgrounds by encouraging them to share and connect through stories. In addition, the Green Card Voices' ***travelling state or national exhibits***, allow for a visual experience with these and others students' journeys, An interactive presentation, these exhibits feature QR links to students' video narratives designed to expand the impact of published collection of personal narratives of their travels to the United States.

Our aim is to spark deep, meaningful conversations about identity, appreciation of difference, and our shared human experience. To learn more about in-person and virtual speaking events, traveling exhibits, and other ways to engage with the *Green Card Youth Voices* stories, visit our website: www.greencardvoices.org.

Act4Change

A Green Card Voices Study Guide

Each person has the power to tell their own story in their own voice. The art of storytelling translates across cultures and over time. In order to learn about and appreciate voices other than our own, we must be exposed to and given tools to foster an understanding of a variety of voices. We must be able to view the world from others' perspectives in order to act as agents of change in today's world.

Green Card Youth Voices is comprised of the inspirational stories from a young group of recent immigrants to the U.S., which they've generously shared with a wide audience. This study guide will provide readers with questions to help them explore universal themes, such as storytelling, immigration, identity, and perspective.

Introduce New Voices:

Participants will select one of the thirty storytellers featured in *Green Card Youth Voices* and adopt that person's story as their own "new voice." For example, one participant may choose Stela Ciko while another might choose Anika Khanam. Participants will become familiar with the life story of their "new voice" and develop a personal connection to it. After each participant has chosen his or her "new voice," read the personal essay first and then watch the video.

Act4Change 1:

Answer the following questions—

1. Why did you select the storyteller that you did?
2. What was interesting to you about their story?
3. What do you and the storyteller have in common?
4. What have you learned as a result of reading/listening to this person's story?

Learn About New Voices 1:

Divide participants into groups of three or four people. Provide each group with copies of the written narratives from five selected stories. Each person within each group will read one of the five narratives. Once finished, the participants will share their narratives with the others. Then, as a group, choose one of the five "voices" and watch that person's video.

Afterward, go on to the journal activity below.

Act4Change 2:

Answer the following questions—

1. What new information about immigrants did you learn from this second storyteller?
2. Compare and contrast the storyteller's video to their story. Which did you prefer? Why?
3. What are some similarities between you and the second storyteller?
4. If this really was your "new voice," what might you want to know about America upon arriving?
5. If you could only bring one suitcase on your move to another country, what would you pack in it? Why?

Learn About New Voices 2:

Each participant will be given a third "new voice." Only one can go to each student; there can be no duplicates.

Inform participants not to share the identity of their "new voice." Participants will try to match their classmates' "new voices" to one of the stories in the book. Encourage participants to familiarize themselves with all of the voices featured in *Green Card Youth Voices.*

Act4Change 3:

1. After they are given their "new voice," ask participants to try and create connections between this third voice and themselves. Have the students read their story and then watch the video of their "new voice." Have them think of a piece of art, dance, song, spokenword, comic, sculpture, or other medium of their choosing that best describes their "new voice."
2. Participants will present a 3-5 minute artistic expression for the larger group from the perspective of their "new voice" in thirty-five minutes. The audience will have a template with a chart that includes each of the twenty-nine *GCYV* students' names, their photo, and a one or two-sentence abbreviated biography. Audience members will use this chart throughout the activities to keep track of what has been learned about each voice that they have heard.
3. Ask the participants to describe the relationship between the *Green Card Youth Voices* and themselves:
    a. What did you notice about the form of artistic expression and the story?
    b. What drew you to this specific art form?
    c. Do you notice any cultural relationships between the "new voice" and the piece of art that was chosen?
    d. What is your best advice to immigrant students on how to succeed in this country? State? City?

More than Meets the Eye:

In small groups, have participants read and watch three or four selected narratives from *Green Card Youth Voices*. After that, have group members tell each other facts about themselves and tell the others in the group what they would not know just by looking at them. For example, participants can share an interesting talent, a unique piece of family history, or a special interest. Then have group members discuss things that they found surprising about the students in *Green Card Youth Voices*.

Think about the "new voice" you transformed in *Act4Change 3*. Tell your group something that was "more than meets the eye" from the perspective of that "new voice!"

For the complete version of *Act4Change: A Green Card Voices Study Guide*, visit our website—www.greencardvoices.org

See also:
Act4Change: A Green Card Youth Voices Study Guide, Workshop for Educators
This workshop is a focused learning experience crafted to deepen teacher understanding and provide instructional strategy, particularly designed to be used in conjunction with *Green Card Youth Voices*.

Glossary

Aibonito: a small mountain municipality located in Puerto Rico

Banyamulenge: the Tutsi tribe that arrived in Congo in the 19th century from Rwanda and historically concentrated on the mountains of High Plateau of South Kivu, in the eastern region of the Democratic Republic of the Congo

Basa fish: a species of fish native to the Mekong and Chao Phraya rivers in Southeast Asia

Bayamon: a municipality of Puerto Rico located in the northern coastal valley near San Juan

Beshbarmak: the national Kazakhstani food made of boiled meat with noodles and onion sauce

Bosphorus or Bosporus: a natural strait in northwestern Turkey that connects the Black Sea to the Sea of Marmara

Consular officer: Foreign Service Officer working for the U.S. State Department assigned to an embassy or consulate abroad

Coup: the forcible overthrow of an existing government from power through violent means often by a small group

Cyrillic: the Cyrillic alphabet is a writing script employed in many Slavic languages across Eurasia, including Russian, Bulgarian, Serbian, and Ukrainian languages

Çubuk kraker: a salty cracker or biscuit, much like a pretzel, popular in Turkey

Dacha: a country house or cottage in Russia, typically used as a second or vacation home

ESL: the acronym for English as a Second Language

ESL Teacher: a teacher who teaches English as a Second Language curriculum

FEMA (Federal Emergency Management Agency): an agency of the U.S. Department of Homeland Security whose responsibilities support individuals and workers addressing the effects of natural and man-made disasters

Fortnite: an popular online video game released in 2017 by Epic Games that focuses on a post-apocalyptic "battle royale," through a fight among many combatants

Fufu: a traditional African dish made from mashed cassava, yam, or plantain, mixed with hot water and made into a paste

Google translator: a free multilingual online service that translates words and phrases between different languages

Green card: a commonly used name for Lawful Permanent Resident Card, an identification card attesting to the permanent residency and work status of an immigrant in the U.S.

Guaynabo: a municipality in the northern part of Puerto Rico, southwest of San Juan

Head Start program: a program under the direction of the U.S. Department of Health and Human Services focused largely on access to early childhood education and health, nutrition and parental support services

IOM (International Organization for Migration): an intergovernmental organization that provides services and assistance to migrants, including internally displaced persons, refugees, and migrant workers

Julio: Spanish word for July

Kange: a simple game played mostly by girls during school breaks. Codified with precise rules, it is played on a pitch measuring 8 meters by 16 meters, marked with a red central stripe and two blue ones on the sides. It's played by two teams of 17 - eleven players and six reserves. A game lasts 50 minutes. It has gradually been gaining the reputation of sport recently. This name is used in the eastern part of the Democratic Republic of the Congo. In the western part, it's called "Nzango" literally means "foot game" in the local Lingala language.

Kakuma Refugee Camp: A UNHCR (United Nations High Commissioner for Refugees) refugee camp established in 1992 in Northwestern Kenya

Kilograms: the base unit of mass in the metric system having the unit symbol "kg," one kilogram equals approximately 2.2 pounds

Kinyarwanda: an official language of Rwanda and a dialect of the Rwanda-Rundi language spoken by at least 12 million people in Rwanda, Eastern Democratic Republic of the Congo and adjacent parts of southern Uganda where it is known as Rufumbira.

Lüleburgaz: a city and district in the western Marmara region of Turkey

Madrastra: Spanish word for stepmother

Madrina: Spanish word for godmother

Muslim Ban: enacted by Executive Order 13769, titled "Protecting the Nation from Foreign Terrorist Entry into the United States," issued by U.S. president Donald Trump on January 27, 2017, prohibiting individuals from coming to the country from seven predominantly Muslim countries

Muyinga: a city located in northern Burundi

NFTA (Niagara Frontier Transportation Authority): a New York State public-benefit corporation responsible for the public transportation oversight of Erie and Niagara counties

Nyarugusu Refugee Camp: a large refugee camp located in Kigoma, Tanzania

Ponce: a large city located on the southern coast of Puerto Rico housing Mercedita International Airport

Ramadan: the ninth and holiest month in the Islamic calendar, where fasting, introspection, and prayer are practiced by Muslims around the world in recognition of the month that Muhammad received the initial revelations for the Quran

Rhombus: a shape having four sides of equal length

Rohingya: an ethnic group, predominantly followers of Islam, living in Myanmar as well as Bangladesh and Pakistan

Shashlik: a dish of grilled meat skewered on a stick, similar to shish kabob

Sukuma: the largest Bantu ethnic group in Tanzania with approximately 10 million members from the southeastern African Great Lakes region

Swahili: a Bantu language and native language of the Swahili people, spoken by 100 to 150 million individuals residing in Eastern and Southern countries, including DRC, Kenya, Tanzania, Uganda, and South Sudan

Tutku: a mini cookie with melted chocolate inside

UNHCR: the acronym for The United Nations High Commissioner for Refugees (aka UN Refugee Agency), whose work focuses on providing critical emergency assistance, including food and shelter to refugees around the world

Urfa: a large city with over two million Kurdish, Armenian and Arab residents located in southeastern Turkey

Visa: issued by a government to grant authorization for an individual to enter another country and remain for a specified period of time; U.S. State Department oversees the issuance of visas to foreign nationals for a variety of purposes, including permanent residency, tourism, business, or transit travel

Yemeni Civil War: an ongoing conflict beginning in 2014 primarily between the Abdrabbuh Mansur Hadi-led Yemeni government and the Houthi armed movement and their allies, both sides seeking recognition as the official government of Yemin; to date approximately 100,000 people have been killed and four million displaced from their homes

Yemeni rial: the rial is the currency of Yemen and as of July 2020, one rial is equivalent to 0.004 USD

Yozgat: a city and the capital district of Yozgat province in the Central Anatolia Region of Turkey with a population of approximately 76,000

About Green Card Voices

Founded in 2013, Green Card Voices (GCV) is a nonprofit organization that utilizes storytelling to share personal narratives of America's immigrants, establishing a better understanding between the immigrant and their communities. Our dynamic, video-based platform, book collections, traveling exhibits, podcast and *Story Stitch* circles are designed to empower individuals of various backgrounds to acquire authentic first-person perspectives about immigrants' lives, increasing the appreciation of the immigrant experience in America.

Green Card Voices was born from the idea that the broad narrative of current immigrants should be communicated in a way that is true to each immigrant's story. We seek to be a new lens for those in the immigration dialogue and build a bridge between immigrants and nonimmigrants—newcomers and the receiving community—from across the country. We do this by sharing the first hand immigration stories of foreign-born Americans, by helping others to see the "wave of immigrants" as individuals, with interesting stories of family, hard work, and cultural diversity.

To date, the Green Card Voices team has recorded the life stories of over four hundred and fifty immigrants coming from more than one hundred and thirty different countries. All immigrants that decide to share their story with GCV are asked six open-ended questions. In addition, they are asked to share personal photos of their life in their country of birth and in the U.S. The video narratives are edited down to five-minute videos filled with personal photographs, an intro, an outro, captions, and background music. These video stories are available on www.greencardvoices.org, and YouTube (free of charge and advertising).

Contact information:

Green Card Voices
2611 1st Ave S
Minneapolis, MN 55408
www.greencardvoices.org
612.889.7635

facebook.com/greencardvoices
twitter.com/greencardvoices
instagram.com/greencardvoices
linkedin.com/company/green-card-voices

Immigrant Youth Traveling Exhibits

Twenty students' stories from each city in the *Green Card Youth* series (Madison/Milwaukee, Atlanta, Minneapolis, Fargo, and St. Paul) are featured in traveling exhibits, available to schools, universities, libraries, and other venues where communities gather. Each exhibit features twenty stories from a particular city, each with a portrait, a 200-word biography, and a quote from each immigrant. A QR code is displayed next to each portrait and can be scanned with a mobile device to watch the digital stories. The following programming can be provided with the exhibit: panel discussions, presentations, and community-building events.

Green Card Voices also coordinates a National Exhibit featuring all six cities. This exhibit is available for rental across the country.

Green Card Voices currently has seven exhibits based on different communities across the Midwest and South. To rent an exhibit, please call us at 612.889.7635 or visit www.greencardvoices.org/programs/traveling-exhibits.

Green Card Youth Voices: Book Readings

Meeting the student authors in-person or virtually helps create a dynamic space in which to engage with these topics firsthand. Book readings are a wonderful opportunity to hear the students share their stories and answer questions about their lived experiences.

To schedule a book reading in your area, please contact us at 612.889.7635 or info@greencardvoices.org.

Order Through Our Distributor

Our books and *Story Stitch* are distributed in the U.S. & Canada by Consortium Book Sales & Distribution, an Ingram Company.

For orders and customer care in the U.S., contact:

Phone: 866.400.5351
PCI Secure Fax (orders only): 731.424.0988
Email (orders only): ips@ingramcontent.com
Online: ipage.ingramcontent.com
Electronic orders: IPS SAN 6318630

Mail: Ingram Publisher Services
Attn: Customer Care
1 Ingram Blvd., Box 512, La Vergne, TN 37086
Hours: Monday–Friday
8:00 am to 5:00 pm CST

For orders and customer service in Canada, contact:

Phone: 800.663.5714
Email: orders@raincoastbooks.com

Green Card Voices Store

Immigration Stories from a Minneapolis High School

ISBN: 978-1-949523-00-3

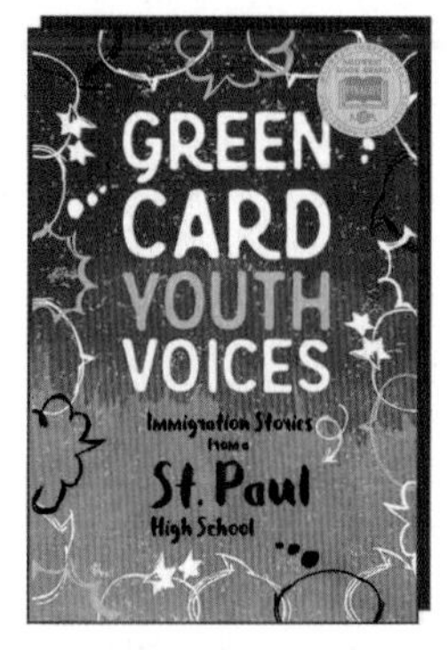

Immigration Stories from a St. Paul High School

ISBN: 978-1-949523-04-1

Immigration Stories from a Fargo High School

ISBN: 978-1-949523-02-7

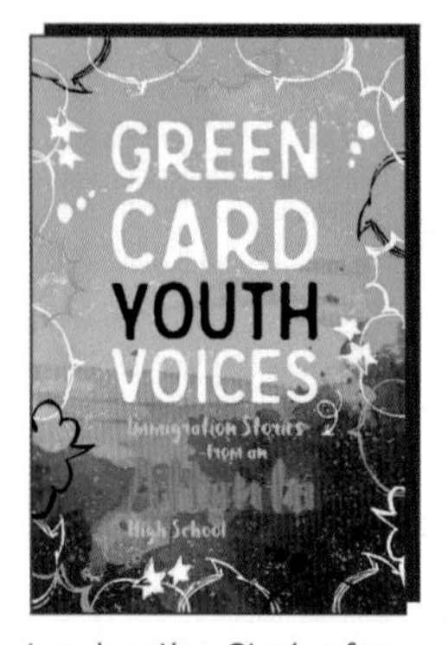

Immigration Stories from an Atlanta High School

ISBN: 978-1-949523-05-8

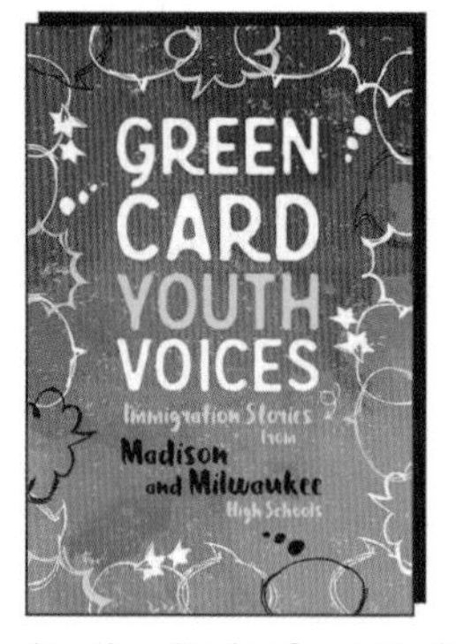

Immigration Stories from Madison & Milwaukee High Schools

ISBN: 978-1-949523-12-6

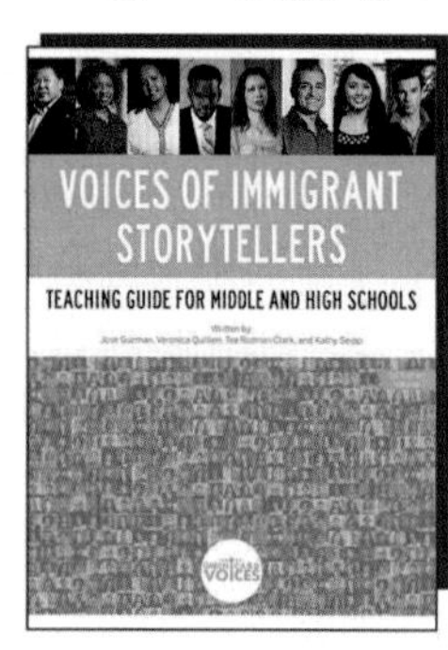

Voices of Immigrant Storytellers Teaching Guide for Middle & High Schools

ISBN: 978-0-692572-81-8

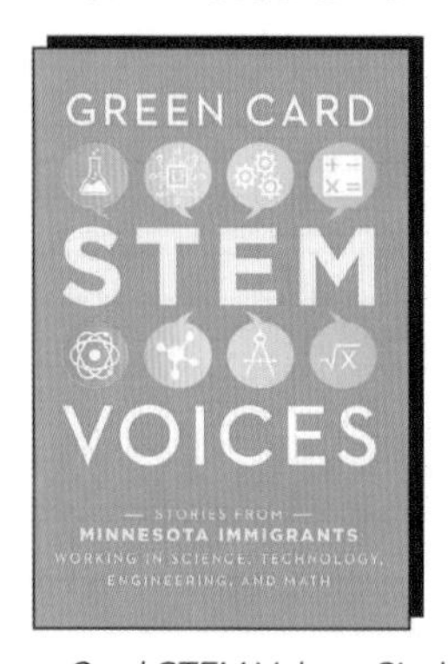

Green Card STEM Voices: Stories from Minnesota Immigrants Working in Science, Technology, Engineering, and Math

ISBN: 978-1-949523-14-0

Green Card Entrepreneur Voices: How-To Business Stories from Minnesota Immigrants

ISBN: 978-1-949523-07-2

Green Card STEM Voices: Stories of MN Immigrants Working in Science, Technology, Engineering, and Math - Teaching Guide for Grades 6-12 and College

Purchase at our online store: *www.greencardvoices.org/store*

Green Card Voices eBooks

Immigration Stories from a Minneapolis High School
EISBN: 978-1-949523-01-0

Immigration Stories from a St. Paul High School
EISBN: 978-1-949523-06-5

Immigration Stories from a Fargo High School
EISBN: 978-1-949523-03-4

Immigration Stories from an Atlanta High School
EISBN: 978-1-949523-08-9

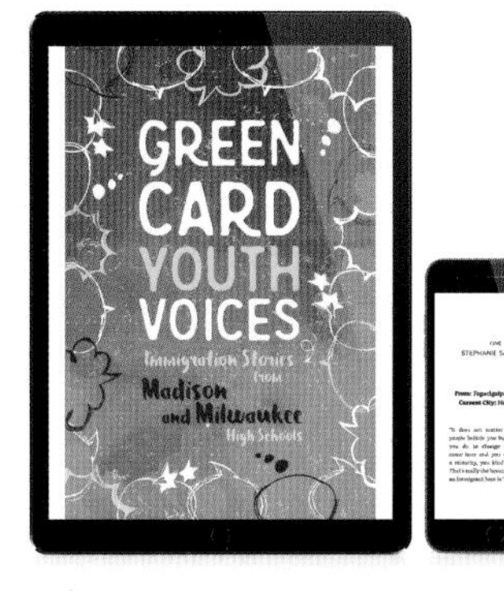

Immigration Stories from Madison & Milwaukee High Schools
EISBN: 978-1-949523-13-3

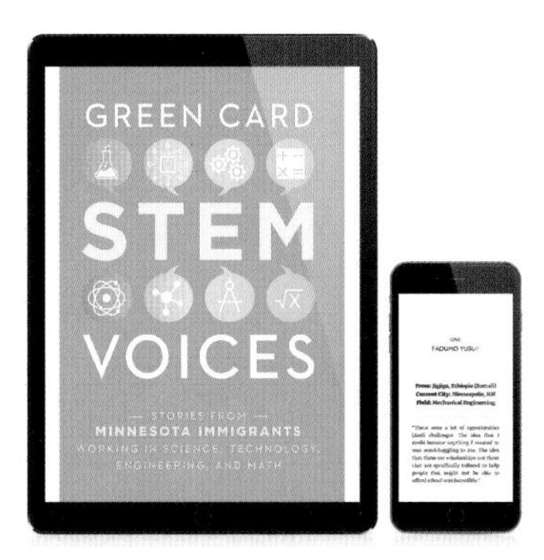

Green Card STEM Voices: Stories from Minnesota Immigrants Working in Science, Technology, Engineering, and Math
EISBN: 978-1-949523-15-7

Green Card Entrepreneur Voices: How-To Business Stories from Minnesota Immigrants
EISBN: 978-1-949523-09-6

Now Available:

Story Stitch:

Telling Stories, Opening Minds, Becoming Neighbors

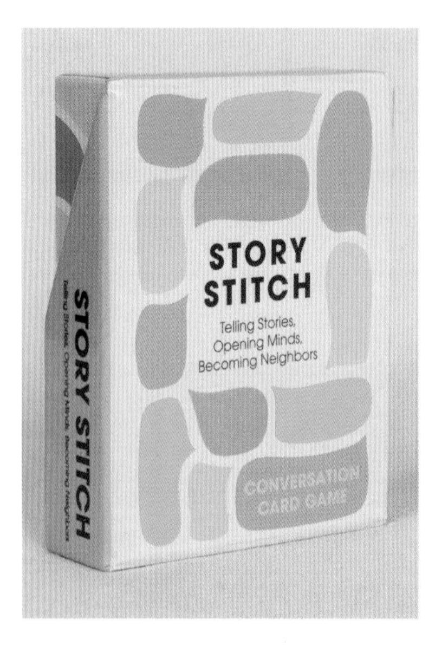

Story Stitch is a guided storytelling card activity that connects and builds empathy between people of different cultural backgrounds. It was created by the diverse Minneapolis/St. Paul community in a series of co-creating game sessions led by the Green Card Voices team. This card game is perfect for: classrooms (ages 10+), diversity training, workshops, work places, leadership / fellow retreats, conferences, elderly homes, and more. Available as a deck (ISBN: 978-1-949523-11-9).

Contents:

- 55 full color, laminated cards
    - 33 story cards
    - 22 stitch cards
- 1 four-sided accordion of instructions

Now Available:

Virtual Story Stitch:

Telling Stories, Opening Minds, Becoming Neighbors

Virtual Story Stitch is a storytelling activity that virtually connects people from different cultural backgrounds and geographic locations by using the Zoom online platform through the computer or phone. It was co-created in March 2020, responding to the COVID-19 pandemic for people to stay connected, share their stories, and feel less isolated during the time of social distancing. There are 33 questions, 7 bonus questions pertaining to the COVID-19 pandemic. There is an abbreviated version with 20 questions total. While *Virtual Story Stitch* can be played by groups of people on their own, the best experience has shown that the best results come when the circles are facilitated by a trained facilitator. A 5-hour long training is provided by Green Card Voices through Teachable E-Course.

Available as a toolkit at www.greencardvoices.org/programs/story-stitch/virtual-story-stitch/

Contents:

- Abbreviated and Extended Story Stitch Questions
- Virtual Instructions Sheet
- Stitch Card PDF and image
- Zoom Technical Troubleshooting
- Informational PDF on Story Stitch

Coming Soon:

Our Stories Carried Us Here:

A Graphic Novel Anthology

This is a bold and unconventional collection of first-person stories told and illustrated by immigrants and refugees living across the United States. Stanford scientist, deaf student, indigenous activist, Black entrepreneur—all immigrants and refugees—recount journeys from their home countries in ten vibrantly illustrated stories. Faced by unfamiliar vistas, they are welcomed with possibilities, and confronted by challenges and prejudice. Timely, sobering, and insightful, *Our Stories Carried Us Here* acts as a mirror and a light to connect us all with immigrant and refugee experiences. Available as an ebook (ISBN: 978-1-949523-10-2) and hardcover (ISBN: 978-1-949523-17-1)

Contents:

- 10 personal illustrated comics
- Cover by Nate Powell, Graphic novelist/illustrator of *Save it for Later, Come Again*, and the John Lewis' graphic memoir, *March*
- Foreword by Thi Bui, Author of *The Best We Could Do*
- Glossary

Also available:

Green Card STEM Voices:

Teaching Guide for Grades 6-12 and College

This unique teaching guide utilizes the perspectives of modern-day immigrants from Africa and Asia. Our diverse storytellers demonstrate the wide range of occupations (chemist, medical researcher, nurse). It is authored by accomplished educators and curriculum developers-including first and second generation immigrants from Africa and Asia—who have added first-hand experiences of the immigration process to each lesson. In line with the National Common Core Standards, these lessons are perfectly suited for grades 6-12, as well as college age.

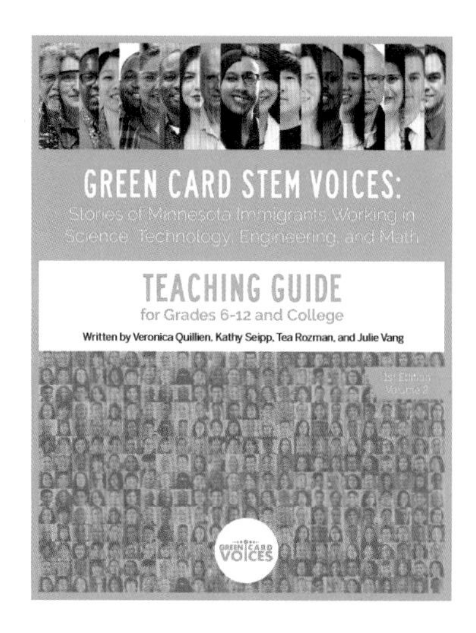

GREEN CARD STEM VOICES:
Stories of Minnesota Immigrants Working in Science, Technology, Engineering, and Math
TEACHING GUIDE
for Grades 6-12 and College
Written by Veronica Quillien, Kathy Seipp, Tea Rozman, and Julie Vang
GREEN CARD VOICES

Available on our website at www.greencardvoices.org/store

Contents:

- 3 user-friendly lessons
- 3 classroom activities
- 3 Green Card Voices video stories
- 3 Green Card Voices essays
- 4 ready to-use worksheets
- 42 illustrated pages

星座